LURE OF THE MANOR

LURE OF THE MANOR

Barbra Baron

First published in 1994 by
Nexus
332 Ladbroke Grove
London W10 5AH

Copyright © James Hallums 1994

Typeset by TW Typesetting, Plymouth, Devon
Printed and bound by
Cox & Wyman Ltd, Reading, Berks

ISBN 0 352 32924 6

This book is a work of fiction.
In real life, make sure you practise safe sex.

LURE OF THE
MANOR

Chapter One

Scion of a famous and most respectable industrialist family, Ellie Branks found herself in serious trouble on that rather chilly, early October evening. The fire in the grate of Miss Petty's austere study was burning low; the headmistress of Chalmers Finishing School for Young Ladies was renowned for her penny-pinching. Ellie had been summoned into the feared presence, her timid rap on Claire Petty's door contested with the single, brusquely delivered word, 'Enter!' She now stood just within the threshold of the study with her slender back to the open door.

For long, silent moments – part of her policy of intimidation towards miscreants – Miss Petty ignored Ellie. Her head, with its carefully piled chestnut hair, bowed, she pretended to pore over a piece of printed paper through heavy, narrow reading glasses. Suddenly, she made poor Ellie jump by grating at her, without looking up, 'For Heaven's sake, shut the door, girl. Born in a barn, were you?'

With great care, Ellie did as she was bade and then, as she was ordered to approach the awesome omnipresence who still chose not to look at her, she shuffled forward, the soles of her flat shoes scuffing on the wooden boards, her delicate hands twisting nervously together at the waist of her long, navy blue, uniform

1

dress. The headmistress allowed her to hover in her misery for a further full half minute on a thin rug in front of her neatly arrayed oak desk. Then she carefully pushed aside the paper, leant back in her swivel chair, steepled her plumpish fingers under her chin and, peering over the tops of her spectacles, sternly surveyed her recalcitrant charge.

The eyes of authority, under other circumstances not unattractive, travelled slowly from Ellie's trim little waist up over a starched-fronted, white blouse – properly loose-fitting so as not to draw undue attention to firm and very full eighteen-year-old breasts – and came to rest on a dismayed, but extremely pretty face with pouty lips, a good, strong, straight nose and wide-spaced, pale blue eyes. Confused by the piercing scrutiny, Ellie looked down at her feet.

With the flat of her hand, Miss Petty sharply slapped the inlaid, green leather top of her broad desk. 'Well?' she demanded, a note of cynicism in her voice, '. . . What have you to say for yourself, Ellie Branks?'

Making tiny, agitated, rocking movements from the waist, not daring to lift her gaze above the level of the desk, Ellie remained silent.

'Cat got your tongue?' The hazel eyes narrowed – but behind her stern façade Miss Petty was beginning to enjoy herself. 'Or swallowed it for shame, have we?'

Ellie noisily cleared her throat as there was another bang, this one louder than the first, the sound of leather against leather, a heavy book hitting the desk top. 'Where did you come by this trash, girl?' the headmistress demanded. Her voice rose several, threatening, decibels. 'Look at it!'

Ellie's milky-skinned Adam's apple jiggled with a nervous swallow as her translucent eyes swivelled upwards and across the desk to the book in question; she bit her bottom lip. Miss Petty flipped open the front cover and found the title page, the grim set of her face completely disguising a pleasurable feeling of rising, lusty anticipation. Ellie still said nothing.

'You will answer me now, by God. Where did you get it?'

Finding a feeble voice, Ellie stammered, 'It, it was at the back of an old cupboard, please Miss. In the, in the art room.' This was not true; it had been going the rounds of the four-to-a-room dormitories, read furtively at night by candlelight, and it had been Ellie's misfortune for matron to discover it tucked under her mattress.

Miss Petty made a show of taking a long, deep breath through flaring nostrils and letting it out as she spoke. 'You found *Justine*, by the Marquis de Sade, in the back of a cupboard in the art room?' she said in utter disbelief. 'It isn't sin enough to read this disgusting, perverted rubbish without compounding your felony by lying?'

Ellie muttered something incoherent to Miss Petty's ears as her tormentor rose behind her desk, dropping the copy of *Justine* onto it with the words, 'There is nothing, but nothing to be said. No excuses.' Her tall, near-voluptuous form swept past Ellie, black, pleated skirt swishing and the heels of her short, black boots clicking as Miss Petty went to the door. Alarmed, Ellie watched as she turned a heavy iron key to lock them in; the girl had heard about this part of the punishment ritual in fine detail – and about what would transpire – from gleeful, previous sufferers only too happy to rub salt into wounds yet unopened. She trembled, unclenching her fingers and resting their tips on the edge of the desk, the foreknowledge of what was inevitably to follow somehow heightening her perception of her temporary gaol with its mellowed, crackly yellow walls and wooden beamed ceiling.

Above the oaken mantelpiece, in central pride of place, hung the bane of Chalmers, a long whippy and well-used cane with a comfortably curved handle, which afforded a most satisfactory grip. Miss Petty moved purposefully from door to chimney, there delaying in order to prolong Ellie's agony by slowly stoking the coals and adding to them. Fresh, bright flames sprung high as she then removed her cane from its hooks with almost reverential care.

Eyes gleaming, flexing her favourite implement with both hands, Miss Petty turned on Ellie. 'Two for reading after lights out,' she told her, barely disguising her relish, '. . . two for lying – and four for daring to read such a filthy book.'

'Please, Miss, no Miss?' pleaded Ellie, with no hope whatsoever.

'Oh, yes, Miss!' thundered the headmistress. Striding over to Ellie she took the fabric of her long-sleeved blouse between finger and thumb just above the elbow and led her by it to a heavy, wooden, early Victorian high-backed chair – her punishment chair – which sat with its back across a corner of the room. Releasing the sleeve, she reversed the chair, as Ellie watched in dread.

'Bend over the back, girl, and flatten your hands on the seat,' Miss Petty commanded. Foolish enough to hesitate, Ellie found her wrist grabbed by the hand holding the cane as the other, tight on the back of her neck beneath her hair, forced her over the chair. The words, 'You dare to defy me, Miss Branks?' spilled from Miss Petty's lips which trembled not in anger

4

but as a result of another, rather more complicated emotion.

The chair was high and Ellie found herself, with her waist tucked over it, standing on her toes. She spread her palms and fingers over the padded, faded brown leather seat where perhaps a hundred or more pairs of female hands had rested before hers. Every little feature of the way her white, thin skin stretched over her bony knuckles was registering keenly in her brain for some reason. As she felt, and heard, her skirt being drawn up over the backs of her legs and folded in a pile on her hips, she bit hard on her bottom lip and screwed her eyes tightly shut. The sound of the cane whistling in the air caused her to tense her backside.

But there was not yet any pain; the swish had been a test run, a flexing of Miss Petty's arm. She stood back a pace. The distance was just right for her to be in no need of her spectacles and she removed them, tucking them into the top pocket of her severe, white cuffed and bodiced black cotton blouse. The transformation was marked and her face seemed more attractive – far younger than its forty summers. Her eyes went on a slow, prurient journey, beginning at Ellie's raised, blue-socked feet from one of which a slipper hung loose, moving up her white, unblemished calves and dimpled backs of her knees to her smooth, shapely thighs, and coming to rest on buttocks whose perfect roundness baggy, navy-blue knickers could do little to disguise. As she ran her tongue over her lips Miss Petty laid the cane lightly across Ellie's behind, taking careful aim; the girl, impeded by the chair-back, tried unsuccessfully to cringe away.

'This is going to hurt,' fell unwelcomely on Ellie's ears, '. . . so remember what it's for – and learn. The

5

first two for reading after lights out.' Except for a spitting coal there was silence and an unbearable ten seconds of waiting as Miss Petty raised her cane above her head and paused. Then it zipped down; the seasoned willow bit and was held firmly in place across quivering buttocks through Ellie's double yelp – the first at the cutting pain and the second at the rush of burning heat.

The headmistress breathed deeply, lifted the cane and brought it down hard once more, trying for the same spot, the excitement in her eyes reflecting emotions most unheadmistresslike which were breaking out within her.

Ellie cried out twice with the next stinging stroke; yet already something other than pain was creeping into her reaction. Her undignified, rudely exposed position and the beginning of the beating together brought to her a feeling which she had not started to comprehend as yet. But aware of a stirring, no more than a flutter, deep in her belly, she opened her eyes to frown at the backs of her hands.

'And now,' growled Miss Petty, '. . . punishment for the lies.'

The cane, fuelled by the full force of Miss Petty's practised arm, lashed twice more across Ellie's clenched buttocks. She no longer shouted – she whimpered. The burning heat which engulfed her backside and seemed to sink into her womb was not, she discovered, unpleasant. Indeed it was a heat which – and she hardly knew this herself yet – was sexually arousing her.

Flickering firelight caused the shadow of an oil lamp to bounce over Claire Petty. The room was barely warm but there was a trickle of perspiration on her unwrinkled forehead. She brushed a straying lock of hair away from her eyes and contemplated the navy-cotton-clad haunches before her. Miss Branks, she noted, was perhaps not making quite such a fuss about her beating as girls usually did; her buttocks were wriggling almost as if eager for the next blow. But, consumed with the wicked excitement of what she intended to do next, Miss Petty attached little significance to this. She slid her hand under the piled skirt onto the small of Ellie's bare back above her knicker elastic. She then bent forward so that she could see the side of the girl's face – or, more precisely, the straight, blonde hair which hid it, falling over the front of the chair. 'The next four swats,' she breathed, '. . . are for the sin of reading smut. A transgression far more serious than the others – and therefore a temptation to be beaten out of naked flesh.'

Ellie turned her head to peer through a gap in her hair at a face she assumed to be distorted in anger, but which was in fact twisted with lust. She observed Miss Petty's eyes narrowing almost to slits as the warm fingers of the woman's free hand slipped under the back of her knickers. As Ellie felt the knickers being rolled down over her bottom, her head-mistress's face disappeared.

Miss Petty leered hungrily at the exposed backside. It had a neat little birthmark in the shape of a diamond on one buttock. She folded the panties over it and eased their elasticated legs down thighs which reacted by closing sharply, knees banging into one another, heels twisting. Ellie meanwhile, blushingly aware of her intimate, blatant exposure, wetted very dry lips. She was overcome by a rush of shame intensified by the realisation of the fact that she was actually enjoying herself.

7

Claire Petty's pussy was a fleshy, furry little animal which had rarely, of late, had the opportunity of being served by a cock; it was not easy for her and her current lover, a married lawyer from the nearby village of Shingley Bay whose offices were in Canterbury, to find mutually convenient times to get it together. She found occasions like this evening's castigation of Ellie remarkably arousing; her speedily ensuing, over-powering orgasm, self induced after a trounced girl hobbled painfully off, was usually at least as rewarding as one brought about by penile penetration. Her eyes latched onto Ellie's beautifully nude, red-welted buttocks and the downy pussy bulge neatly framed between their lower curves and the tops of her thighs. She craved to touch, to finger and grope the fleshy mounds, to invade the virgin cunt lips; but such behaviour was, of course, prohibited to the head-mistress of a finishing school who was properly administering sound and just punishment; so only her eyes trespassed.

She again raised the cane, savouring this moment more than any previous one. Detecting movement, Ellie swivelled her eyes upwards. For the first time, she saw the shadow of the raised arm and cane, grotesquely distorted, angled into the corner of the room high above her head. The shadow dipped and disappeared as, in the instant, springy willow had its initial taste of naked bottom. Ellie yelped. She jerked her abused behind so hard that her hips knocked the heavy chair forward an inch to bump the wall. Her dress slid down her sloping, nobbly spine to enclose her head and shoulders in a tent and as it did so, before the echo of her shout had died, the cane lashed down to bite into her once more.

Buttocks burning and throbbing, libido itself consumed with fire, Ellie, almost without being aware of it, was knocking and rubbing her pussy into the chairback whilst contracting and relaxing the muscles of her vagina. She sobbed – not from the pain of the flogging as Miss Petty, her own pussy tingling, assumed, but in reaction to the deep and powerful stirrings of orgasm. Until these delicious moments, masturbation had been Ellie's sole means of satisfying her burgeoning sexuality; she had not even indulged herself in those hidden, much whispered about, smutty activities with other girls. Now as the cane sang through the air and connected for the seventh, and then the final slash, her orgasm swept through her, causing her to shudder from head to toe, her knees and elbows turning to jelly; then she went as limp as a rag doll.

Miss Petty was panting. Her pussy throbbed with need. Reluctantly lowering her cane, she inspected the damage it had inflicted. Ellie's poor bottom was not cut but burnt fiercely around the edge of the brightest of the angry welts. Her shapely, crimson, glowing buttocks were peppered with tiny bruises which all but obliterated her diamond birthmark. The headmistress, mightily pleased with the results of the beating, sighed raunchily – yet another bottom had been thoroughly dealt with, another saucy young lady put properly in her place. She was perhaps fortunately not aware that sexual juices were seeping from Ellie's contented vagina to soak into the bush between her tightly-closed thighs; neither could she see the beatific expression on the girl's face because it was covered by the rudely rearranged skirt.

Craving now for self-fulfilment, with shaky hand Miss Petty hung up her cane. Her brow perspiring, she took a last, lingering and most salacious look at her handiwork before pulling up Ellie's knickers and covering her with her skirt. She was now so keen to get rid of Ellie in order to frig herself that she failed to notice as she took her by the upper arm and straightened her that the girl was in a state of post-orgasmic euphoria. She marched her to the door, sent her out into the passage, and, banging the door closed, locked herself in.

In somewhat of a daze, hands over her dress cradling and rubbing her raw and tender backside, and marvelling that its heat was capable of penetrating knickers and fabric, Ellie wandered off towards the dormitory.

Trembling, Miss Petty flopped down into the chair behind her desk. She bunched her black dress and white petticoats over her waist, dropped a large pair of white cotton camiknickers to her dimpled knees and shoved two probing fingers deep inside her very wet pussy. She began a furious masturbation as, with her free hand, she fumbled on her spectacles then reached for the confiscated copy of *Justine*. Flipping the book open at random on the flat of her desk, she happened by chance on one of its most sadistic passages – the same description which had most aroused Ellie the previous night.

Her eyes widened as her fingers moved even faster.

Chapter Two

That very morning, Jeremy Brexford – a lord by right of inheritance since the untimely demise of his father one year before, on Jeremy's thirty-eighth birthday – had taken delivery from London of a high-powered telescope. The young Lord Brexford, with money to burn, was constantly seizing upon new ways of amusing himself; astronomy, he had decided the previous week, was to be his latest hobby – though it was doubtful it would ever reach the obsessive proportions of his interest in the motor car, or of his consuming passion for sex.

The Brexford ancestral home, Deal Manor, a grey and rather forbidding-looking Gothic pile whose exterior – and in particular several of the flying buttresses – was in some need of the attentions of a stonemason, dominated the top of a gentle hill. On the far side of a dense wood – part of its grounds – between Deal Manor and the sea, and in clear view of it, stood the mid-Victorian country house which had recently become Chalmers.

Shortly after nightfall, on the evening that Ellie Branks was to discover that caning can induce sexual bliss, Jeremy was busily installing his telescope. He had chosen one of the many unfurnished rooms occupying the third, and upper, low-ceilinged storey of the manor because it had a large skylight. He worked from a book of instructions on a table at his side. Next to this lay a pamphlet on the sky at night – about which at this point in time, he knew next to nothing.

Once the simple workings of the telescope were mastered, Jeremy spent several minutes exploring the mysterious and pitted surface of the almost-full moon. Then he straightened up to run an admiring eye over the smooth lines of the five-feet long, nine inches across at its widest, gleaming copper contraption itself. His eye was drawn to a window, attracted by the light of the moon glinting on the restless English Channel on the far side of the wood and the cliffs. Then his gaze fell on Chalmers, standing near the clifftop, most of its windows illuminated by the light from gas or oil lamps.

With its houseful of near-as-damn-it imprisoned young ladies being groomed in all the social graces whilst long since – in Jeremy's not incorrect view – having passed the age of sexual awakening, Chalmers had of late occupied much of his libidinous thoughts. That such a feast of luscious young virgin flesh should be within a short canter from the manor and yet unobtainable, was becoming an almost insufferable irritation.

His gaze drifted from the finishing school to his telescope. To hell with the stars! In that instant, he discovered his probable subconscious reasons for having developed a sudden, unexpected interest in astronomy. His thin lips, housed in an ascetic face as lean and well-put-together as he himself was, tightened into an anticipatory smirk. Widely spaced, slightly droopy eyes of deepest brown, creased at the edges. He ran a hand through his wavy black hair then swung the telescope down, from pointing at the skylight, to the direction of Chalmers. Stooping to the eyepiece, he readjusted the focus.

Several minutes, and windows – many of them with curtains disappointingly closed, others with nothing remotely interesting going on behind them – later, the front lens of Jeremy's telescope swivelled to the upstairs, uncurtained windows of Miss Petty's study. The room had two large sash windows, stretching from floor to ceiling with small, wrought iron balconies in front of them in the Victorian fashion. The power of Lord Brexford's telescope was such that the effect when trained upon the study was just as if he were standing on one or other of those balconies himself.

He discovered Claire Petty sitting behind her desk, working at something or other. He explored the room, was amused at the dominant positioning of the cane over the fireplace, and, quickly bored, was about to continue with his general scan of the school when the gorgeous Miss Ellie Branks timidly entered the headmistress's study.

From that moment on until, half an hour later, Miss Petty collapsed in a sprawl over the words of the Marquis de Sade with her fingers relaxing inside her wet and oozing pussy, Jeremy's attention remained fixed on the wholly unexpected, wonderfully libidinous scene. Then, sporting a hard-on which threatened to burst its way out of his breeches, he went urgently in search of his young wife.

Sophronia Brexford, twenty-two, was a bride of just seven months. At the moment of her husband's hasty departure from the skylight room on the floor above her, she was seated in front of her dressing table, her svelte figure clad in a pink, floor-length

13

housecoat with flared sleeves. The glassed surface of the table was cleared of its usual collection of face paints, creams and powders, and in their place were arranged various objects of cabbalistic significance. The centre-piece was a skull with rubies set in its eye sockets. There was a pair of crossed bones, a silver chalice containing red wine, a silver bell, some beads and, providing the only light in the bedroom apart from that cast by a roaring fire, two black candles in golden holders. In lipstick amongst these things was a crudely drawn magic square, each of its rows and diagonals of numbers totalling fifteen. And in the middle of Sophronia's forehead, in the same lipstick, she had painted a large eye.

As Jeremy quietly entered the room unnoticed, Sophronia – her thick and wavy dark hair, with its reddish glint, spread over her shoulders – was staring at her reflection and repeating firmly to herself, over and over, 'Every day, in every way, I am getting better and better.'

'At what exactly, may I ask?' murmured Jeremy, as he crept up on her from one side.

Startled, she gave him an admonishing smile. 'You shouldn't interrupt me like that,' she told him. 'I'm building confidence in myself so that my magic powers can grow.'

'Ah.' He laid a hand on her shoulder, his eyes latching onto her beautiful, emerald green eyes in the mirror, piercing them, lust very close to their surface. 'And how about your sexual powers, my love?' he asked her as his narrow, strong fingers squeezed her elegant shoulder.

She raised an eyebrow, giving him a crooked smile. 'I understood you found those fairly well developed?'

'I find this fairly well developed.' He bumped his

14

loins into her side just behind her elbow, jabbing his erection into her ribs.

Her mouth forming a delightfully surprised 'Oh,' she reached behind her to slide her fingers over his bulge and grope it. 'Exactly what brought this on?' she asked huskily.

'My new telescope. I was experimenting with it, having a look at Chalmers. I chanced upon the most extraordinary thing.' He rocked his hips.

'I see.' Sophronia curved her palm and fingers lengthways over Jeremy's straining cock, stroking it through his trousers. 'A naked wench, was it?'

'Better. A bare-arsed thrashing.'

Her eyes lit up. 'My, my. Lucky you!' Turning on her padded chair to face him, she released his cock from the pressure of her hand and body and reached for his top trouser button. 'And now, of course, you expect me to do something about this naughty thing of yours?'

'It needs,' Jeremy told her, the words sticking in his throat, '. . . the administration of your pretty mouth.'

Very slowly, eyes and hands ribaldly savouring her actions, Lady Brexford undid her husband's fly buttons. 'Penis worship,' she muttered, tongue dampening her fleshy lips, '. . . happens to be on my list of the occult for study – and practice, dear heart.'

Beneath the trouser buttons were more buttons, for Jeremy was wearing long, woollen-mixture underpants which fastened down the front – no problem for his lady who, in any case, took a risqué pleasure in the gradual revelation and release of her favourite plaything. With both sets of buttons undone, trouser and pants' fronts gaped over an unruly mat of curly black pubic hair; amongst this was barely visible the wide base of Jeremy's cock, it's length trapped to one

15

side, but Sophronia's hand went in, fishing. Wrapping her fingers around her husband's warm, thick, solid hard-on she dragged it into the candlelight. As her fist jerked on its silken skin, her free hand crawled deep into his crotch to tug out from under the vee of his underpants balls that were heavy and swollen with semen they longed to release.

Keeping a possessive hold of Jeremy's begging tool, Sophronia opened the top of her gown from neck to waist, stretching its glossy fabric on either side of her not over-large, but finely moulded, breasts, and rubbed the purple glans of her captive cock over each teat in turn. Her wide, pointy nipples, as deep a red as the glint in her hair, hardened in response. Holding the stretched foreskin fully back down his shaft – for His Lordship was uncircumcised – she tormented his cockhead by flicking her tongue at it like a frog catching flies, and by squeezing a minute part of its tip into the tiny glans hole. Then she took his testicles, one after the other, fully into her mouth before licking his cock from balls to head and finally sucking as much of it between her lips as her mouth could accommodate.

Watching both Sophronia's blow-job – performed with an expertise perhaps beyond her years due to his skilful coaching – and its reflection, Jeremy fought for control. The memory of the caning stamped vividly in his mind, extremely excited both by his secret witnessing of the event and now by Sophronia's fingers, tits, lips and mouth, he felt an orgasm build almost to the point where there could be no holding back. He longed to flood his gorgeous mate's mouth, to see his seed trickling from its corners and down her pretty chin. But Jeremy was the son of a hedonistic father who in his day had revelled in laying half the country, and had inherited his sexual traits – especially, to the delight of his wife and of his countless conquests, that of drawing out a wanton scene to the very limit of his staying power.

By a supreme effort of will, Lord Brexford held back his climax. Cupping Sophronia's face in his hands as if picking up a rugger ball, he drew it up and away from his loins, whilst his cock – wet with her saliva and responding to his will – hovered below her chin. He looked at her, she looked at him and raunchy, knowing laughter flashed between their eyes. She was aware in the long seconds of silence which ensued that she should not touch him in any sexual way, that these moments were crucial for the protraction of this latest little episode in their extremely successful and highly unconventional love life.

He released her face, letting his breath out very slowly and, rigid cock just perceptibly throbbing with his heartbeat, he unbuckled his slender belt and slipped it free of its trouser loops. His trousers fell baggily to his knees, where he let them stay. Feeling the need to have Sophronia restrained – that only in such restraint would he remain in full control of this libidinous situation – he held the long belt in one hand as he stripped the gown off her shoulders and down to her waist. She watched only his cock, fascinated by it as it jiggled with his movements whilst he pulled her arms forward slightly, wrapped the belt around her torso, threaded it through the buckle and pulled it very tight. Imprisoned thus, crushed together and uplifted, her breasts seemed far bigger than they were. Moving in to them, his need to ejaculate dominant, Jeremy worked his cockhead between the two rolls of tit flesh and drew it in and out in a fucking motion.

17

But one belt hardly makes satisfactory bondage. Searching in the folds of gown at Sophronia's waist, Jeremy found an end of her sash and pulled it free. She murmured, her first words since before enclosing his cock in her mouth: 'I was supposed to be learning about magic.'

'Another kind of magic,' he grunted, securing her wrists and knotting the end of the sash around them. 'And how you love it.' He touched a finger to the red eye on her forehead. 'What is this?'

'Evil eye,' she said.

'Keep it away from my prick.'

He kicked off his shoes and struggled out of his trousers and underpants, but made no move to remove his short, tight, loose-sleeved shirt. 'You look remarkably vulgar like that,' she told him, nostrils flaring, gaze, yet again, riveted on his genitals. 'You could be somebody's stableman.'

He undid a button, but she stopped him by insisting, 'Keep it on Jeremy – I like you looking dirty!'

'And you, my love, are a remarkably smutty young lady.' Closing in on her, he took hold of the trailing end of the sash and looped it around the back of her neck, under her hair. He pulled on it so that her tied hands were lifted to reach her chin and made another knot; her breasts were now squashed sideways, hard nipples poking out between folded arms.

With the end of the eighteen inches or so of sash still loose, Jeremy pulled Sophronia to her feet. The housecoat dropped down her legs into a heap on the rug and she was naked, except for soft, silver slippers. Her lushly thick vee of pussy hair had about it a similar coppery glint to the hair of her head. Keeping a firm grip on the sash, and clasping her buttocks with his other hand, Jeremy dragged her into him so that his hard-on dug into her belly, flattening upwards against it as his balls settled comfortably into her pubic thatch. He put his lips, slightly apart, against her mouth, his tongue probing to find hers; but he did not kiss her.

'In a while, I'm going to put my prick inside your cunt,' he mumbled into her mouth. He jerked his hips with almost savage force, knocking her back a pace along the front of her dressing table, '. . . but you're going to have to wait for it.'

He pushed her once more then stood back from her, tongue tip protruding through a slackening mouth, eyes twitching; in such moments he had the ability to appear almost saturnine – a fitting companion for her occult studies. Then, after a preliminary tug on the sash, he hauled her to her ornamental brass four-poster bed to send her sprawling across its crimson coverlet with a rough shove. She rolled completely over her tied hands and arms to lay still on her back, facing him, her parted legs offering him a splendid view of her pussy. Breathing shallowly, she opened her lips to run her tongue over her pearly white, sharp little upper front teeth. 'You, My Lord, are a *bastard*!' she flung at him.

'And you, a witch.' Clambering onto the bed, he straddled her breasts and, with his big cock hovering over her nose, he took the end of the sash and secured it to the brass bedhead; it ran, tautly, up one side of her face and through her hair. As he was completing this task she raised her head to tongue the skin of his dangling scrotum between her teeth, and nipped it hard enough to cause the tiniest flash of pain. He gasped, then, lifting a knee over her and rolling away with an expression of mock outrage, he clasped his balls in both hands, and said, 'You will pay dearly for that!'

19

On occasion, when the mood took them, the couple enjoyed watching one another masturbate, the sight of their actions often spurring them on to mutual orgasm. Understanding how keyed-up his wife was at this moment, and how under slightly different circumstances this could have been just such an occasion, Jeremy determined on a fitting torture for her in her bondage. Taking a fancy-edged, white linen pillow from beneath the coverlet, he propped his back against it on the bottom corner-post of the bed, making himself comfortable. His legs were fractionally apart and flat to the bed, a foot touching the outside of one of her slippers, his cock proudly pointing at the canopy above it, and his balls hanging heavily between his hairy thighs. Folding a hand around his hard-on he began lazily to stroke it, noting smugly the burning lust in her eyes as she watched him.

In a soft and husky, almost hypnotic voice he talked dirty to her, describing to her the scene through his telescope, but blatantly embellishing what he had observed. He had Miss Petty going down on Ellie Branks to bring her off as she bent over the chair and then obliging her charge to do the same as she perched on the corner of her desk, hands entwined in Ellie's hair, dress and petticoats pinned up high by her elbows. The further into his inventions he got, the faster became Jeremy's masturbation, and the more Sophronia squirmed and wriggled against her bondage, rubbing the inner tops of her thighs desperately together, thereby trying in vain to bring relief to a thoroughly needful pussy.

As the black candles burnt lower and the fire sputtered brighter, Jeremy continued this mischievous torment of Sophronia with relentless self-control, bringing himself several times almost to the point of climax, then pausing, recovering, and repeating the procedure, equally as turned on by his actions as Sophronia, who, aching to get a hand to her pussy, was both inflamed and frustrated by them. She begged and pleaded for sexual contact for almost half an hour, to no avail.

At this point Jeremy, having tortured himself considerably as well as her, fell upon her. But he did not untie her hands or unstrap her arms. Kneeling between her legs, he lifted her loins off the bed, slipped his thighs beneath her and, on his haunches, with her knees resting over the crooks of his elbows, and her feet dangling in the air behind his rump, he pierced a pussy soaking from prolonged need with a cock which was itself begging for ultimate relief.

The fuck was short, frantic and glorious. With her buttock flesh crumped into fiercely clutching hands, Jeremy used Sophronia's bottom to heave her up and down on his hard-on, banging his hips as if riding a bumpy horse, whilst she frenziedly joggled hers, her feet leaping and bouncing loosely at his back.

Moaning, gasping, squealing, wanton emerald eyes locked on the mingling pubic bushes and the fast appearing and disappearing root of the cock buried between them, Sophronia came, wailed – and fell silent but not still, because Jeremy was going through his final cortortions, throwing her up and down his shaft until, accompanied by a triumphant shout, his hot seed flooded her pussy. He lifted her and dropped her once more, shot into her again, then again before keeling over onto his side, taking her with him by her buttocks and their locked genitals, as a final dribble joined her pussyful of sperm.

Lengthy moments later Jeremy became rather less aware of their steadying heartbeats – his hand was tucked beneath Sophronia's left breast on top of the belt – and quietening breathing, and more aware of the longcase clock in a corner of the bedroom, whose excessive tick he found mildly irritating, whilst she insisted it lulled her to sleep. He opened his eyes and lifted his head to peer above her face through her disarrayed hair; it was ten minutes past seven. Cook would no doubt be wondering why they had failed to appear for supper.

They were sexually joined, still. Sophronia was, apparently, asleep, still firmly secured with her arms pinned to her side over her breasts, and her tied hands tucked under her chin. Her body was angled away from his at the waist. Easing back his hips he watched his flaccid cock, damp, fat, flopping out of her to brush a thigh, leaving a smudge of sperm as he pulled away. She made a tiny grunt of protest at the break in intimate contact.

'Awake, then?' he observed; she had a tendency to fall into a brief but deep sleep after sex.

'Mmmm.' Her eyelids came fractionally unstuck as he rolled off the bed and went to stand with his bare buttocks to the fire, looking at her.

'You might untie me now?' Sophronia wriggled her hands and opened her eyes fully. They were attracted, inevitably, to his genitals; seven months of marriage – and five months of riotous screwing before it – had done nothing to lessen her fascination with them. She adored him like that, with his neatly done-up shirt and the rest of him naked; in its way, it was deliciously sordid.

'I might, yes.' He smoothed his hands over his backside, enjoying the way the heat from the fire spoiled the backs of his legs and his buttocks. He was far from cold, but the five-century-old pile was beginning to be invaded by an encroaching winter, with its early warnings of a bleak chill to come. Walking to the window, he stopped to rest his fingertips on the broad, stone sill, gazing through leaded panes across the oak and beech wood and down to Chalmers, with its several dozen lighted windows. He was unsure, without the telescope, which belonged to Miss Petty's study.

'I wonder who that woman was?' he asked the moon.

'The lady with the cane?' Sophronia surmised.

'Exactly. She wasn't at all old. Rather good looking, too.'

'Maybe it was Miss C. Petty,' she suggested, admiring his lean, strong buttocks whilst at the same time turning and twisting her hands in a vain struggle to free them. 'Will you please set me loose?'

He left the window and ambled towards the bed. 'Who is that?'

'The headmistress. The name is up on a board outside the school, and she was pointed out to me in the village. She's sort of mid-thirtyish and a bit plump, with brown hair.'

'That sounds like her, yes.' Kneeling on the bed, he unbuckled the belt and slipped it off her, then fought the knots in the sash, which had become tight. 'She is somewhat of a fiend, is Miss Petty.' The first knot submitted and he unlooped the sash from the bedhead. 'She gets very turned on from caning a girl on the bare derrière.'

'So do you, my heart,' Sophronia reminded him.

'Indeed.' Her wrists were still firmly bound and as he got off the bed, he tugged the sash and pulled her arms forward. She sat up, then was quickly obliged to swing her feet to the floor and stand up, to avoid being pulled flat.

'Dearest, please?' she weakly protested as he again went to the window, taking her with him.

He pulled her in close, like a man tugging a boat by its mooring rope, then wrapped an arm around her shoulder, tipping his chin towards Chalmers. 'After the chastised girl was dismissed, Miss Petty masturbated. I didn't tell you that, did I?'

'You told me a number of dirty things. I don't remember.'

'Ah – but they weren't necessarily true, do you see? There was no cunnilingus. She simply submitted the young lady to a most sound thrashing, sent her away, then frigged herself.' Jeremy's hand crept down Sophronia's bare back to her bottom, and slipped low under her buttocks from where he inserted his fingers into her still wet and warm pussy.

She wriggled happily. 'And watching that gave you a marvellous cockstand.'

'Precisely.' His fingers unplugged her pussy; it was, after all, well past supper time; one hunger had been assuaged, another was becoming more pressing. As he began to release her wrists he muttered, 'I wonder what the "C." stands for?'

' "C."'? What "C."'?' The sash fell away from her hands and she gently pressed the only minor welt resulting from her bondage, on her wrist just below the ball of her thumb.

'Miss *C.* Petty, you said?'

She smiled disarmingly at him, wickedness tempting her as so often. 'Maybe it stands for cunt?' she suggested most sweetly, as she grabbed a handful of his genitals.

He grinned down at her. 'That mouth of yours is . . .'

'Yes?' she challenged, interrupting, squeezing.

'Most pretty, my dear.' He unprised her fingers, finding the renewed excitement they were bringing him inconvenient at that precise moment. Besides, he loved to call a halt to sex play whilst there remained the desire for more – it was rather like putting aside a good book at a gripping moment; one could hardly wait to get back to it.

With a last, lingering look towards Chalmers, Jeremy said, 'I must see to it that we get together socially with Miss C. Petty as soon as possible. I imagine she will prove most entertaining, as well as . . . useful.'

'All those young ladies?'

He smacked her bottom hard, the sound of it echoing in the high-ceilinged room. 'You are possessed of a most grubby mind, Sophronia,' he told her. He glanced down at his rudely exposed genitals and at her nakedness. 'Perhaps we should dress for supper – what say you?'

Chapter Three

Weekends, unless Jeremy Brexford opted to drive up to London in search of adventure with some of his seedier friends there, were usually occupied with house guests. This particular Saturday only three were expected. The amiable and somewhat perverse Edwin Smythe-Parker was bringing down two of the most popular, attractive and sexually athletic good time girls of London. The fact that their origins happened to be the East End did nothing to make them less sought after by playboys of the upper classes.

Smythe-Parker, celebrated novelist, almost as much of a literary society darling as Wilde had been before him, arrived with his disreputable companions at Deal Manor late in the afternoon, borne splendidly in the very latest model Rolls-Royce automobile. His chauffeur, sitting in the open driving section, bundled up like an Eskimo against the chill, made a showy business – as instructed – of roaring right up to the steps of the manor then slamming on his brakes whilst sounding the powerful klaxon horn at the same time. Drawn to the drawing room window by the racket, Sophronia with him, Jeremy perceived that the young ladies were as glamorous as Edwin had promised they would be.

Millie was first to emerge from the car, tucking

straying locks of her piled-up, flaxen hair under a little black hat, whilst smallish, blue eyes gazed in awe at the rambling Gothic pile to which she had been brought. She made the mistake of taking her overnight bag with her instead of leaving it for a flunky who hurried – too late – to open her door. Lettice, with strong, darkly handsome features which suggested Indian ancestry, and with heavy black hair hanging straight to her waist, spilled out the other side amidst a flounce of petticoats, exhibiting an undignified amount of black-stockinged calf above short, button-up boots. Edwin, with his baleful eyes, his slight limp and neatly trimmed black beard and curly moustache, was on Lettice's heels, a hand mauling her behind; a man who could always be relied upon to ferret out the most desirable of women, he had been between the two and had savoured certain of their delights most of the way from London.

Flinging a woolly scarf around his neck and thrusting broad, gloveless hands deep into his greatcoat pockets, Edwin cast a quick eye over the manor. 'Here we are then,' he said cheerfully; 'bit scruffy here and there on the outside but quite charming within.'

'Scruffy?' repeated Millie, shaking her head in disbelief. 'That what you call it? It's a bleedin' palace!'

Lettice, who at least had the education to allow the flunky to bring her bag from the Rolls, seemed less impressed. She glanced at the huge front doors, one of which was open. 'Where's Lord Whatsit then?' she asked.

'Jeremy? He'll be around somewhere. But he probably won't appear for a while,' Edwin told her.

A shadowy figure behind lace curtains not far from them, Jeremy was scrutinising the charms of the young ladies. 'Not bad,' he muttered approvingly to Sophronia, 'not at all bad.'

Lady Brexford made appreciative noises. 'I must say I rather like the look of the yellow-haired one,' she said.

Her husband grabbed and squeezed her buttocks through the thin, russet velvet of her ankle-length dress as the two of them watched their weekend visitors approach the stone steps which swept grandly up to the doors. His hand dug deeply under her bottom, scrunching the velvet. 'By which I take it you would like to dally with the wench?' he asked.

It had taken Jeremy Brexford a mere three months of marriage to train Sophronia – who had in any case been fully aware of and captivated by his scandalous ways and reputation when first they met – for the sort of behaviour he expected from a wife. It appealed to the natural wantonness within her that she should be a pliable sexual plaything, willing, indeed happy, to indulge in group sex and mild degrees of sado-masochistic behaviour with him – little more in that respect than a slave; that their excesses together should sometimes include her making love to a member of her own sex whilst Jeremy looked on, or joined in, merely added spice to the carnal pie.

However, there was one strict proviso in this smorgasbord of sex. Whilst it was perfectly all right for Sophronia to be caressed carnally by men and to caress in turn, and whilst it was encouraged that she should lay her hands on their naked genitals, it was absolutely forbidden that their cocks should penetrate her most intimate places; that is to say her vagina, anus and mouth were out of bounds for any penis save that of her husband. This prohibition she found at times exceedingly frustrating; it was the kind of refined form of torture at which Jeremy was most adept and which ultimately heightened her craving for his body.

Sophronia clenched her buttocks tight against Jeremy's groping hand and thrust her hips forward towards his probing fingers as Millie disappeared into the great hall. 'I'll need to have a good close look at that girl,' she wickedly told him, 'and discover if her hair is naturally that colour.'

'Of course you may have a thorough inspection of her fanny, dirty lady,' he said, 'and quite shortly, I imagine.' His fingertips thrust as hard into her pussy as her protecting skirt and knickers would allow and then, to her regret, departed.

Millie's abundance of silken pussy hair was indeed shot with flaxen tones, an agreeable fact which Jeremy was first to discover after a short and boozy supper. Before they ate he had briefed the wanton young women on what might be expected of them sexually after supper, warning them that he and Lady Brexford were possessed of most devious brains, and that Smythe-Parker – a fact of which they were already delightfully aware – had a highly acrobatic imagination. As a reward for their compliance – not that they would not willingly have thrown themselves into the weekend without one, with utter abandon – he had promised them splendid new outfits from one of the capital's most renowned couturiers.

When, at supper's end, Sophronia showed Edwin and Lettice into the richly furnished drawing room, where a huge fire roared in a massive, grey stone chimney, Jeremy took Millie into a small, cheerless and chilly room. There he obliged her to strip off all her clothes except for a black, whaleboned corset, which shoved her breasts high to expose half her nipples while its pleasingly shaped bottom perfectly framed her almost skinny buttocks and her well used, flaxen-streaked fanny.

Unconcerned about her nakedness, but bothered by the cold which brought goosebumps to her flesh and seeped into the soles of her feet through the bare, flagstone floor, Millie was shivering with her arms wrapped around herself as Jeremy produced from a voluminous pocket of his jacket what appeared to be a leather dog collar and leash.

'What the 'ell's that for then?' Millie asked suspiciously. They were the last words she was to utter for some while. With a glint in his eye, but no explanation on his lips, Jeremy rolled the widish band of leather around her lower face, easing an affixed, broad rubber plug between her teeth and buckling the affair tight around the back of her heaped-up hair. The leash was clipped to a little metal loop on the other side of the rubber plug at the centre of Millie's mouth; the contraption was one of many such devices beloved by Lord Brexford, specially made to order for him by a leather worker with a little shop just off Jermyn Street, in London.

Jeremy led Millie by the leash out of the room and into a draughty corridor. By the time they entered the drawing room her feet were numb with cold and she was shivering, her skin beginning to turn blue; only the tight rubber plug prevented her teeth from chattering. He took her straight into the heat of the fireplace area where the other three were awaiting her expectantly. Edwin was perched with Lettice on one of the two soft and tasselled sofas which flanked the chimney. Sophronia, having just heaved a pine log the size of a strong man's thigh onto the flames, shifted to one side so that Jeremy could stand Millie in the centre of the hearth.

All eyes latched onto Millie's deeply scooped, trembling buttocks as she warmed herself, her face on a level with a row of pewter mugs which hung along the front of the grey stone mantelpiece. As she rubbed her palms vigorously together, her knees shook as if she desperately needed a pee. Edwin gloated, Sophronia smirked and Lettice, wondering what fate was in turn to be hers, looked on excitedly.

Jeremy now put his little invention to a second use. After threading the leash through a leather loop at the back of Millie's head, near the buckle, he turned her back to the fire, removed a mug from its hook and attached the leather end of the leash in its place. When Millie felt the need to move away from the fire there would be only enough slack to allow her a pace forward off the hearth; for the moment, gooseflesh and blue tinge receding, life creeping back into her feet, she remained as close to the flames as she was able.

Standing back from Millie, Jeremy surveyed her with a cynical, thin-lipped smile which he then turned on the others. 'Sophronia,' he told them, 'had occasion to wonder aloud earlier whether Millie's fanny hair matched that of her head.' His eyes darted to the whore's corset-framed loins. 'As we can all now observe,' he went on, 'it does – very nicely.'

'How perfectly splendid,' muttered Edwin, cock stirring beneath his trousers.

Jeremy took a step towards her and groped the inside top of Millie's thigh, hand hooking into it, little finger with its diamond ring almost touching her pussy. He tugged her legs apart, saying, as he did so, 'The female pudendum, source of so many of man's problems. From the Latin *pudenda*, meaning the shameful parts.' His hands slipped up an inch, the side of the pinkie sinking into pussy flesh. 'Are you ashamed of your cunt then, Millie?' he asked her.

She answered with a negative shake of her head, brittle-blue eyes staring curiously into his. This lord was treating her in a manner most strange and abusive but, knowing it was but a game, that the abuse was not for real, she determined to get into the swing of things. So far she was only slightly turned on. Trussed and subjugated by the mouth, having been miserably cold and now turning decidedly warm, blatantly exposed, she was uncertain how her libido was reacting. Awkward and a little detached, yet, having offered her body for the weekend, she was resolved to receive as much pleasure as she could from what was to befall her.

Jeremy's hand left her thigh to cup her chin, fingers pinching her cheeks. 'Not ashamed,' he said. 'Good. Then open it up for us, why don't you?' He let go of her to join Sophronia who had settled into the sofa opposite Edwin and Lettice; Edwin, he noticed, was toying with Lettice's breast over the top of her embroidered cambric bodice.

Heat was beginning to sink into Millie's bottom and the backs of her legs. She moved forward off the hearth onto a patterned rug, shifting herself as far as the tight stretched leash would allow from the flames. Then, in obedience of Jeremy's request, her thin hands slid down over the black corset, and scarlet-nailed fingers met inside the tops of her thighs to take hold of her pussy lips and pull them apart.

'Bend at the knees and thrust forward your hips,' Jeremy ordered. 'Let us all have a good look inside there.'

Edwin pulled Lettice's hand down onto the now very solid bulge beneath his fly buttons as he ogled, enjoying a good eyeful of Millie; she meanwhile performed with appropriate lewdness, swinging her loins in Jeremy and Sophronia's direction. As she re-arranged her grip on her vulva to open it fractionally wider, she decided she was beginning to get a kick out of being the vulgar centre of attraction.

'Look how pink the flower is,' Jeremy muttered to Sophronia. 'Pink petals and a red and mysterious centre. And see how the hairs which surround it are darker than the rest.'

Sophronia smiled greedily, licking her lips. 'She's very, very nice,' she murmured.

Laying a hand on his wife's velvet-hidden crotch, as he suggestively probed there, he picked up a silk cushion and offered it to her with raised eyebrow. 'I'll wager the strumpet tastes nice, too,' he said. 'And I'll bet you can't wait to sample her.'

Emptying the contents of a champagne glass down her throat, Sophronia chuckled throatily and left the sofa, taking the cushion with her and dropping to her knees on it in front of Millie. Grasping the girl by very warm buttocks, she closely perused her open pussy before leaning in to it and dipping in her tongue. Millie, for whom this sort of female genital caress was a rare event which she found more arous-ing than the often ineffective slobberings of those of her lovers who were that way inclined, gasped. She rocked her hips. Her hands moved from her vulva and she entwined her fingers passionately in Soph-ronia's soft blonde hair. The muscles of her inner thighs twitched against the cheeks cushioned between them. Her pussy very quickly became wet.

'I say, Sophronia?' Lady Brexford, too engrossed in her cunnilingus to heed her husband's words, slid her tongue deeper into a cunt whose taste she was finding most sweet.

'Sophronia?'

Reluctantly unmouthing her prize, Sophronia turned her head to find that her husband was leaning forward and offering her a quarter-full champagne bottle.

'Of course, you are well aware what I'd like to see you do with this?'

Indeed she was. Giving Jeremy a slack-mouthed, wet-lipped smile she took the bottle. After up-ending it and swallowing a copious draft she carefully inserted the neck into Millie's vagina. Holding the bottle by its broad base she eased it up as far as it would go without causing undue stretching – two-thirds of the way down the sloping shoulders – and began jiggling it there whilst, with the fingers of the other hand, she toyed in the girl's buttock cleft.

Smythe-Parker's handsome cock, large and sturdy like himself and almost as famous, was now standing upright through unbuttoned trousers, tufts of pubic hair of a similar hue to his beard bunched around its base. Lettice's nimble, mauve-nailed fingers were wrapped around it, lazily wanking him. Jeremy meanwhile, though hard himself, restrained an urge to free his straining cock as he divided his prurient attentions between Millie's 'bottling' and Lettice's hand-job, noting that Edwin's arm was buried to the elbow beneath Lettice's skirt and crinoline petticoat.

With her fingers entwined in Sophronia's hair, her legs well spread and the leash taut between the back of her head and the mantelpiece, Millie randily observed the rude penetrations of the Moët bottle. The sport was not new to her; it was one of the favourite practices of a regular, wealthy lover of hers and normally left her unmoved. But her pussy had been most excited by the attentions of Sophronia's mouth, and the wanton lady was even now teasing her bottom crack and its tiny hole in a manner that sent tingles through her bowels. Millie, despite the fact that she was getting somewhat hot, was beginning to be as turned on as perhaps she had ever been.

'Enough,' Lord Brexford pronounced suddenly. He held out his hand as Sophronia stilled hers and turned her head to look at him. 'Give me that,' he muttered.

The bottle made a slight sucking noise as it was withdrawn; what was left of the champagne sloshed. Taking it with a leer, Jeremy made a business of sniffing and licking its neck before upending it in his mouth and draining it with a show of relish. Then he tossed it, Cossack-style, over one shoulder. It smashed on a flagstone in a corner, the noise echoing in the room.

Lettice's mouth replaced her hand on Edwin's cock. As she avidly sucked, he dragged her skirt and petticoats up her legs until they rested in an untidy heap on bare, dusky thighs above red-gartered, black stocking-tops. Groping up to her hips beneath the pile he grabbed the waistband of lightweight linen knickers. As she raised her bottom to aid him, he eased them down to her knees, over her shins and off one foot, leaving them loose around one booted ankle.

Edwin, who would eat any pussy including that of a whore, picked Lettice's legs up and flattened them against the sofa. Clambering onto his knees behind her head, he pushed his trousers and underpants down his muscular thighs, pulled her clothes onto her waist, handled his cock into her mouth and folded himself down on top of her to bury his bewhiskered face in her crotch.

Thus visually stimulated, Jeremy now found the need to unloose his hard-on irresistible. He first removed his jacket, shoes and socks, then stood up, dropped his trousers and stepped out of them. He was not wearing underpants, and his erection stood like a potent staff at the open bottom of his shirt; he restrained the urge to lay a hand on it.

Now the only member of the company not to be genitally exposed, Sophronia was caressing Millie's pussy. She had it cupped in a crabbed hand, her index and middle fingers buried within up to the second knuckles. Her face tucked into the girl's swannish neck, she was sucking on it, producing a love bite as Millie squirmed and made loud grunts through her gagged mouth – not only the result of Sophronia's raunchy attentions but also because the heat of the fire was becoming a little uncomfortable on her backside and legs.

It was perhaps fortunate that Jeremy chose that moment to peer at Millie's bottom and decided to save it from burning. He parted Sophronia from her, unhooked the leash, slipped it free of the loop at back and retethered her, facing the flames, but mercifully further away. 'Just look at her Edwin,' he sighed. 'Such an interesting sight.'

The author raised his head from Lettice's pussy and, moustache glistening, turned his gaze on Millie, whose buttocks and the backs of her slender legs had turned an appealing shade of pink all the way from hips to calves, a clear demarcation line between the pink and white of her flesh. Flattening a hand against her buttock, Jeremy found it pleasingly hot to the touch. He closed in on her, warming his cock in her bottom cleft, working it upwards as he reached his hands around her and yanked down the top of her corset to cradle her breasts.

Mightily turned on, craving to remove her clothes but not daring to until so requested by His Lordship – one of his group sex rules – Sophronia sank down onto the vacant sofa, trying to watch the activities of both couples at the same time. Edwin's face was once more cushioned between Lettice's thighs as they lustily went about their sixty-nine.

Eyes flitting from Edwin and Lettice to her husband and Millie as Jeremy buttock-fucked the girl, Sophronia bleated, 'Why don't you do her properly, darling?'

'Why not? A quickie will make a change, will it not?' he responded raspingly. 'A little warm-up.' Pulling Millie's hips back as far as they would go from the fire, so that she was half bent at the waist with her hands on the mantelpiece, he spread her thighs. With the back of his cock pressed into her vulva he grated, 'You put it in for me, Sophronia.'

'May I then take my clothes off?'

'You may not – until I say so.'

Frustration rising toward unbearable heights, Sophronia left the sofa and did her husband's bidding. Reaching between his legs she took hold of his cock, coaxed his hips off Millie's backside with her free hand, and worked Jeremy's glans between her pussy lips. Gripping Millie's nipple area in much the same fashion as he would hold the reins of his horse, Jeremy thrust his cock hard into her with a loud grunt, the brusque action knocking Sophronia's hand down his shaft to catch hold of his balls.

Thus began one of Lord Brexford's rare quickies. As, nearby, Lettice gobbled Edwin towards climax, the lordly buttocks embarked on an intensive pounding. He made Sophronia squat beneath Millie, her back to the fire, and lick both her clitoris area and his balls each time he was fully impaled. Millie's knuckles were raised high, the pads of her fingers very white on the rough stone mantelpiece. Her head was wobbling, beginning to shake her hair down, her eyes were glazed and fixed – without registering – on a hunting print. As the fronts of her thighs started to tingle and heat crept through her corset, the muscles of her vagina went through a series of strong contractions, spurring her sexual assailant towards a rapid end to his unusual but greatly enjoyed knee-trembler.

Jeremy came with a bellow like that of a bull elephant, his first climatic heave almost knocking Millie into the chimney as Sophronia rocked back on her knees beneath them. His seed poured into Millie's pussy and her vagina milked him as it went through a final, powerful contraction. As he lurched into her to shoot his final drops, she shuddered and produced a mixture of moans and pleasure noises through her gag. He went very still as Sophronia, arm bouncing beneath her rucked-up skirt, fingers furiously working in her pussy, flicked her tongue tip over his testicles.

Seconds later, Edwin ejaculated into Lettice's mouth and rolled slowly off her, a second eruption splashing her cheek and lips as he collapsed by her side. Lettice swallowed Edwin's sperm with relish, thoroughly enjoying, as always, the musky taste, the sticky texture. At a peak of libidinous pleasure, she dropped a hand onto her black-bushed pussy and sighed contentedly.

Jeremy's cock, wilting but still formidable, flopped wetly alongside Sophronia's pert nose as he withdrew it from Millie. Sophronia's urgently jerking fingers had brought her almost to climax. She began to make mewling sounds, but her husband let go of Millie's tits, took Sophronia by the elbow and dragged her hand from beneath her velvet skirt as he pushed himself fully upright.

Sophronia wailed protest. She banged her thighs and knees together. Lord Brexford extended her torture.

'Later,' he told her. 'Save it.'

As Jeremy moved away from Millie, who but for the heat of the fire would have sunk to her knees in front of it so surprisingly intense had been her orgasm, he pulled Sophronia to her feet. Her pussy was throbbing with need. Her rumpled skirt fell to her ankles. At that moment, with her craving for climax overbearing, she experienced real resentment. The knowledge gained in experience of her husband's quirky ways, that this enforced frustation would eventually lead her to a most rewarding orgasm, did little to soothe her.

'This isn't fair, Jeremy,' she complained as she was taken between the sofas, out of the fireside area, with his fingers digging sharply into her elbow. 'Why should you, and they . . . and not I . . .?'

'Your mouth,' he interrupted, 'is often so much sweeter firmly shut.' His words were merely a part of mildly sadistic play-acting.

'And you, sir, are a scurvy whoreson,' she responded.

He grinned. 'An unspeakable bastard, no?'

'A vile worm!'

Stopping them beside the gramophone, he let go of her arm. Despite her irritation she could not help sneaking a peak at his shrunken cock, but she resisted the urge to handle it.

Indicating a pile of brown-sleeved records, he told her to play something for them. This was not exactly what she needed at that moment, but at least the occupation might fractionally take her mind off her pussy and its ferment. She wound the spring of this relatively novel addition to the modern world up fully, fixed a new steel needle in the pick-up head, put the first record which came to hand onto the spinning turntable and carefully fitted the needle in the groove; through the massive, chrome horn there emerged the sounds of Scott Joplin's piano as the inventor of ragtime played 'Reflection Rag'.

Sophronia's next thought, as her eyes fell on the bottles of champagne lying on a small rack, cool on the stone sill of an arched window, was to get properly squiffy. Picking up a bottle, she stripped the wire from its neck and began wrestling with the cork.

Millie was in a certain amount of trouble. Her tits, hanging close to flames which leapt ever higher, were getting rather hot as her buttocks had earlier; her nipples were starting to feel as if they might burn. As the champagne cork leapt from beneath Sophronia's thumbs to fly across the room and land near Millie's hand on the mantelpiece, she was grunting her discomfort as loudly as the rubber plug would allow, and straining her head against the leash. This time, as he tapped his bare foot in time to the music and watched Edwin slowly sitting up as Lettice pulled her dress and petticoats down to her knees, Jeremy failed to notice Millie's plight.

The girl was obliged to release herself or scorch; her hands scrabbled with the tethered leash. At that moment, Edwin was fastening the top button of his trousers, though his flies remained gaping; for some reason, the fact that three of the five were more or less dressed, even Millie wearing her whaleboned corset, had filled Jeremy with an urge to be completely naked. His shirt was off and sailing towards the sofa as Millie clumsily freed herself and reeled backwards into his arms.

Jeremy's hands closed over Millie's breasts, bra cups drooping below them. His genitals, cock still damp from her juices, bumped into her buttocks. 'My, my,' he muttered, 'a hot young woman indeed. I don't recall permitting you to release yourself, but I quite see why you needed to.' He momentarily roughened the pinky breasts then let them go to undo the buckle of her gag.

'Could I please 'ave a drink?' gasped Millie as soon as the rubber plug was out of her very dry mouth.

Sophronia, having drained one glass of champagne as fast as its fizziness permitted, refilled it along with another which she took to Millie, who quaffed thankfully.

'What am I then, a bleedin' leper?' mumbled Lettice, sitting up and stretching out a hand.

Jeremy produced a smile of tolerant benevolence. Comfortable in his nakedness, he left Millie and padded to the champagne rack where he took another bottle and began to open it. 'We shall all thoroughly refresh ourselves,' he said as 'Reflection Rag' came to its lilting, slightly stilted end. 'My lady wife will turn the recording over, and we shall further enjoy the delights of Mister Joplin, filling our ears with music whilst we tickle our minds with alcohol and then . . .' His eyes flickered, amused, towards Sophronia as she fitted the gramophone needle into the track of a number called 'Elite Sincopations', '. . . and then we shall, all together, see to Sophronia properly. She is in extreme need of sexual relief, Her horny Ladyship.'

Chapter Four

At eight in the evening, as up on the hill Lord Brexford opened the third bottle of champagne and caught its spewing foam expertly in a glass rather than, as his wife had done with the second, spill it over the floor, Ellie Branks found herself alone in her four-girl dormitory with one of her sleeping companions, plump Georgina. Unbeknown to Ellie, her chubby friend – no saint, who had once dabbled in the hay with one of Deal Manor's stable lads – had recently developed a serious case of the hots for her.

'Pru and Toots won't be back for quite a while, not until just before lights out,' Georgina pointedly remarked, referring to their dorm-mates who were beginning rehearsals for the end-of-term play.

Ellie, who was lying on her tummy on her bed, reading and kicking her feet in the air, at first took no notice.

'You and I will be alone together for at least an hour,' Georgina said, standing near the head of Ellie's bed, looking down at her. Ellie glanced up sharply from her copy of *Jane Eyre* – which she would far preferred to have been the confiscated *Justine*.

'And what of it?' she asked with a frown.

Georgina brushed fleshy fingers through crinkly hair the colour of walnuts. Sensing that a blush was about to rise over her barely seventeen-year-old cheeks she turned towards the window, glancing up beyond the copse at the moonlit manor, wherein more ribald acts had taken place than her mind, prurient though it was, could conceive of. 'Oh, it was, it was just that . . .' She stammered. 'Oh, God, forget it, will you?'

Puzzled, Ellie, in her nightdress, stared at her friend's back, its appealing pink meatiness barely discernible through her school blouse. Putting the book down flat with its pages open on the brown wool coverlet of her bed she said, 'There surely has to be something up with you Georgie – what's this big thing you're making about us being alone?'

Moving hesitantly to the window, Georgina stooped to turn up the gas fire. She looked around at Ellie and bit nervously on her bottom lip before telling her, 'I . . . I've been thinking about your caning.'

As had been Ellie – very much so; it was the reason she was reading on her stomach and had also been the cause of a furtive, dawn masturbation. She found Georgina's confession most surprising. 'And what about my caning?' she asked.

The girl straightened up, facing her, the annoying blush in retreat. 'It must have really hurt, no?'

'I told you that yesterday when I came back. Naturally it hurt, stupid. It hurt like hell – and still does.'

'I've never been caned.'

'It's only your second term. Just you wait; Petters is bound to find an excuse to lay into you.' She paused, then said archly, 'I've got an idea that the cow likes it.'

'It was hardly an excuse in your case. That shocking book.' Georgina had read only one brief passage and that had made her blush from head to toe. She was biting her lip again, eyes speculatively resting on the area where the skirt of Ellie's nightdress fitted tight in a pleasing curve around her bottom. 'Are you bruised and stuff – there?'

'Gosh, you want to know some things, don't you?'

'Well – are you?'

Ellie laughed at her, but the laughter was short lived as she noticed an expression she wrongly interpreted as concern in the hazel eyes which continued to dwell on her backside. 'I'm sore, yes,' she told her.

'Did you put anything on it?'

'No.'

Georgina had forged her opportunity; she had dared. She told herself to be firm, not to allow Ellie to refuse. She went to her cupboard and produced a small tin. As she approached the bed she was unscrewing the top. 'This will do you no end of good – do let me soothe your behind for you,' she said, trying to keep her voice from shaking.

Surprised, Ellie asked her what it was.

'It's a balm – for healing.' She sat sideways on the bed which sagged and creaked under her weight, and, reaching determinedly for the hem of Ellie's nightdress which was bunched into the back of her knees, began to pull it up.

'Um, I'm not so sure that you should . . .' muttered Ellie, very slightly alarmed at Georgina's behaviour which she would have found extraordinary had not her friend seemed so genuinely sympathetic.

But the nightdress was already up – at least, the back of it was – heaped above Ellie's baggy, navy knickers which totally obscured her buttocks and the damage they had suffered. Georgina's fingers slipped under the elastic of their waistband. This action was pushing things a step too far for Ellie who protested, sweeping the invading hand away with her own.

'I can't make it better if you won't allow me even to see it!' grumbled Georgina.

'Well, all right. But I won't have you taking my knickers down. Here.' Despite certain reservations, Ellie was beginning to find Georgina's behaviour amusing. Her cheek fell flat on the bed as she used both hands to pull her knickers tight up into the crack of her behind, fully exposing the sadly bruised and battered buttocks.

'Wow!' exclaimed Georgina, most impressed. 'She didn't half give you a beating, didn't she?'

The overall glow of red had faded, but each stroke of the cane had raised a welt on one buttock or the other, or across both, welts of a purply, angry blue.

'What does it look like?' asked Ellie who had had no chance all day to examine her rear end in a mirror.

Georgina, who from the start of this girlish attempt at seduction had been lusting for a sight of Ellie's bottom, found its mauled appearance most arousing now that it was exposed so close to her. Touching a welt with the tip of a finger, she traced it from its six inch start to its end. She almost replied that it looked gorgeous, but stopped herself, instead saying, 'It's very hurt, poor thing. Poor you. But don't worry, I'll help it to get better.' Dipping three fingers in the tin of whitish cream she scooped out a generous amount and smeared it over Ellie's left buttock.

Her behind had been bothering Ellie all day, smarting, throbbing and heated, a constant, uncomfortable reminder of both pain and pleasure. Georgina's touch was most gentle and the cool, smooth cream began instantly to assuage. As pudgy hands went caressingly to work, palms moving in small circles to make flesh quiver, Ellie settled down with a contented sigh, resting her chin on the backs of flattened hands, closing her eyes, wiggling her toes, as yet unaware of her dorm-mate's dishonourable intent. As the unguent was worked into her pores, good feelings began to arise within her; the centre of her existence became the soothing of her backside.

Handling the so-desired flesh caused Georgina's nostrils to flare and her eyes to narrow. Her first objective was achieved; the second, that soft, secret place which lay hidden below tender cheeks and between the delicious tops of white thighs, just beyond where wisps of curly pussy hair peeped from under the narrow roll of knickers, was very close; Georgina was most determined to reach that virgin place.

As if to encourage her friend's wanton ambitions, a small shudder of content went through Ellie; her bottom wriggled happily beneath Georgina's deft hands. Directly below Ellie's crotch, there happened to be a slight bulge in the mattress where a spring was insisting its way upwards, and as her pubis rocked with the wriggling of her bottom, she became aware of this. An event in Georgina's favour, Ellie's wobble induced a tremor in her pussy.

Hands became more daring. Fingertips extended beyond the path of damage to where the cane – at least, applied as it had been from the side – could not possibly have reached. The white tips of neatly manicured nails found their way between the buttock mounds as far as to come into contact with the thin knicker roll and slid lower, until they touched some straying pubic hairs. Goal almost achieved!

The thumbs arrived first. Changing tactics, Georgina spread her hands over Ellie's hips and moved them down and towards each other, over the buttocks to their underswell, thumb tips closing in on one another, brushing pussy hair and moving on to meet together, nail to nail, on the soft roll of heavy fabric exactly where it covered Ellie's vulva. A distraction from her real purpose, Georgina squeezed the buttocks as her thumbs probed to put gentle pressure on yielding pussy lips.

For a second, Ellie froze. Her eyes sprang open. Her pubis stilled on the hump in the bed. Slowly, she twisted her head to look back over her shoulder at Georgina's slack-mouthed face. Their eyes locked, Ellie's puzzled, a little troubled, Georgina's softly lustful, a very leading question plainly written in them. Both girls remained statue still.

Georgina produced a most tenderly encouraging smile. Since Ellie had failed to jerk away from her so obviously sexual touch, she dared herself on. The thumbs crept beneath knickers to meet again, this time on soft, naked pussy lips where they intruded up to the knuckles to discover dampness.

A sharp intake of breath from the industrialist's daughter. A pussy clenching, unintelligible mutterings. Submitting with a sort of libidinous wonderment, Ellie again wriggled her crotch against the hump beneath it and closed her eyes.

Full of confidence now, very wet between her legs, Georgina speedily stripped the obstructive knickers down Ellie's legs and off. Index and middle fingers replaced her thumbs to slide into Ellie's pussy as far as they would go, way past the little fold of hymen. Laying down beside her, she kissed her cheek and ran her tongue up to her ear as she withdrew her fingers to their tips then plunged them in again three times. She whispered, 'Nobody ever did this to you before, did they?'

'Nobody but me,' sighed Ellie.

'Like it, don't you?'

'Mmmmmm.'

'I'm going to do something to you now that you couldn't possibly do to yourself.'

Ellie's body, rather than her mind, decided that she was going to submit willingly to just about anything at all. Georgina's fingers left Ellie's vagina, and she turned her onto her back. Her hands slid under her upper thighs to raise her hips slightly, and she slipped a pillow under them. Then she got down on her knees on the worn rug at the foot of the bed. Flattening her torso between Ellie's parted legs, she examined the prize thus presented to her inches from her nose; tenderly parting its lips with finger and thumb as her free hand climbed up under her own skirt and inside her knickers, she poked out her tongue to plunge it deep into Ellie's sweetness.

Hardly able to believe the ecstatic feelings which were beginning to course through her, Ellie gasped – and gasped again. Not content with fucking her like a little prick, Georgina's tongue paused between each series of plunges to trace a wet path along her perineum to her bottom hole, where it briefly dipped before returning to pussy.

Waves of pleasure threatened to overwhelm both girls. Georgina, instinctively proficient at it as she may have been, had performed cunnilingus only on two previous occasions. The taste and smell of Ellie's fanny, and the sight of the underside of her bruised and welted buttocks drove her fingers wild inside herself, and her tongue wild within Ellie. Mutual orgasm rushed upon them.

This was the precise moment when Miss Petty chose to make one of her sneaky little inspections. Walking quietly down the dimly gaslit corridor, she distinctly heard a girlish sigh and a soft moan. Pausing at the door from behind which these sounds had come, and there hearing more of the same, she very slowly and cautiously inched it open a hand's-breadth – which was sufficient to afford her a clear view of the bed and the most wanton activity being enacted upon it.

Claire Petty's eyes opened perhaps wider than they had ever done in her life. She scarcely dared to breathe. The bed had begun to creak rhythmically to the movement of Ellie's rocking, bouncing buttocks. Miss Branks's head was ecstatically rolling. Her hands had found their way between her thighs and Georgina's torso, and she was kneading and squeezing the girl's fat tits. Miss Petty could tell who Georgina was only by her generous figure, since her face was hidden in the tops of Ellie's thighs. Georgina's body wobbled in time with the creaking springs, and the hand stuck up her skirt was in a feverish state, making the fabric draped over her wrist leap and jiggle.

The headmistress of Chalmers greedily studied every detail of the girls' actions for a half a minute; their revelations would be stamped in her mind for a lifetime. Then Georgina emitted a groan muffled by Ellie's pussy, her fingers stilled within herself and Ellie's loins arched tautly off the pillow, taking her first ever lover's face with them. As orgasm ripped through her, for some deep, dark, salacious reason Ellie moaned words which reached clearly to Miss Petty's incredulous ears. 'Oh yeeees,' she sighed, 'beat me hard. Lash me. Lash me!' As Ellie fell silent, her thighs closed tightly around Georgina's face and her feet crossed in the small of her back. Miss Petty, who, for some twisted logic of her own did not want to be discovered, most carefully and quietly closed the door.

As she wandered off down the deserted corridor in somewhat of a daze, the headmistress dwelt ribaldly on what she had seen and heard, and considered how she could turn her exciting, new-found knowledge to her advantage. So Ellie Branks, the little slut, had actually been pleasured by her caning, had she? Of course, she realised, she would have noticed this had she not been so absorbed in her own enjoyment; on reflection, the girl had certainly acted rather differently from the other punishment victims. Then an opportunity must be found at the earliest possible moment to subject Ellie to another, severe, whipping – perhaps under circumstances even more lubricious than before. And the smutty Georgina deserved to have her fat behind treated to a thrashing she would never forget.

Chapter Five

As Georgina, who was suffering the sort of guilt pangs which often engulf boys needlessly after masturbation, unmouthed Ellie – who on the contrary enjoyed a feeling of content repleteness mixed with wonder at this second revelation of her offbeat sexuality within twenty-four hours – up at Deal Manor, Lord Brexford was draining his champagne glass. Edwin Smythe-Parker, still dressed, but with his fly buttons gaping, fetched the bottle to replenish both their glasses as Jeremy fixed a speculative eye on Sophronia, who had just finished rewinding the gramophone.

Sophronia changed the steel needle and dropped it into the groove of a piece from the 'Brandenburg Concerti'. Feeling her husband's gaze upon her, as the music somewhat scratchily filled the room, she looked up at him; there was a hornily speculative look, the meaning of which she knew so very well, on his face.

'You might now find it amusing, my dear,' he told her, 'to occupy yourself with removing whatever items of clothing any of us are still wearing.'

Her expression challenged his. She jutted her chin stubbornly; the master and recalcitrant slave game which they both so enjoyed playing was clearly about to continue. 'I might. Then again, I might not,' she responded. But her pussy, its pleading for fulfilment having barely abated, experienced three tiny contractions of excitement.

Jeremy ignored her affected obstinacy. 'I have decided,' he went on, 'that you will begin with Edwin – if he harbours no objections that is?'

'Not at all,' said Edwin, his bearded face affecting a lopsided grin. Moving to the fire, he put his back to it and took a long swig of his Moët before placing the glass on the mantelpiece. 'I am at your disposal dear lady – you may have your evil way with me.'

Sophronia's eyes swept in apparent indifference over the assembled company, and came to rest on her reclining lord and in particular on his fine genital set which nestled slackly between slightly parted thighs. 'As a matter of fact,' she said to his penis, 'I find myself weary. I do believe I shall take myself to bed.'

His face tightening into lines of mock anger, his eyes hardening, Jeremy pushed himself to his feet and approached her, cock swaying. He grabbed her fiercely by her upper arm. 'You will do exactly what I tell you,' he hissed.

'Kindly unhand me, sir,' protested Sophronia, but with little conviction in her voice and making no attempt to brush his hand off. 'You exceed your husbandly authority.'

'Have you so soon forgotten your sacred marriage vows? You swore, if you remember, to obey.' Pulling her hand behind her, he turned her towards Edwin then pushed her to him, forcing her to her knees. 'You will begin,' he said, unhanding her, 'by bringing Edwin's prick and bollocks into the light. He has already done half the job for you, as you can see.'

Sophronia stared in frank and prurient interest at

the open fly and underpants buttons; beyond them an inch or so of Edwin's cock was visible, its base buried in his thick pubic bush, the rest of it tucked into his pants. As she momentarily reassumed her pretence of reluctance, she tore her eyes away to glare up at her husband. 'You have a most disgusting mind,' she told him. She turned her look of distaste upon Edwin. 'Both of you do. Men can be so revolting.' But then her eyes slithered down over his buttoned waistcoat to fall on her hands as, with a wanton smile, she pulled the fly front wider apart and fumbled open the rest of the underpants buttons.

She cupped her hands to fish behind Edwin's warm genital packet with all her fingers. Rather as if she were lifting a bowl of water to drink from it she brought cock and balls out together and held them very close to her face. Edwin's flaccid cock, near enough so that if she stretched her tongue she could have licked it, drooped between her wrists. Teasingly, she slipped the tip of her tongue through her teeth and wiggled it, eyes rolling lasciviously to meet Jeremy's. 'Shall I then suck it, lord and master?' she scornfully asked, words and attitude a deliberate extension of their game, for she knew that this act, except with her husband, was forbidden her.

'Should your lips dare to go the slightest bit closer to that prick,' he grated, 'you will find yourself punished by being chained nude in the wine cellar for the entire night.'

In truth, Lady Brexford was sorely tempted to commit the forbidden act; the cradled balls were warm and trembly in her palms, and the fat cock was showing encouraging stirrings of life. With a sign of regret she relinquished Edwin's genitals, opened his belt and the top button of his trousers, yanked off his shoes and, keenly aware of the stiffening cock whose glans was rising towards her chin in a series of tiny jerks, got him out of his lower clothing. Clambering to her feet, with the author's penis growing as it dug into the russet, velveteen belly area of her dress, she finished the job of stripping him naked.

Lord Brexford was quite a hairy man, but in comparison, the hirsute Edwin resembled an ape. Standing well back from Edwin, he took his champagne glass from the mantelpiece and commenced to empty its contents, his cock now achieving maximum size. Sophronia swept ribald eyes over the two naked men. Edwin gave her little time for such sexual speculation. 'Now Millie,' he ordered.

There was not much of special excitement to be revealed in the denuding of Millie since she was wearing only the black, whalebone corset, her nipples already free over the bra and her pussy, which had in any case been thoroughly perused by all present, naked below the crotch. The corset laced up down the front and despite the fact of her slimness, Millie's vanity had dictated that she squeeze herself in very tight. When Sophronia worked the laces loose, it fell apart to expose her hips as being faintly, puffily red from their enclosure.

'S'pose it must be my turn now, then,' mumbled Lettice. She leaned forward and stretched a hand to the hearth, depositing her empty glass on it, her hair falling to the rug as she did so; her knickers hung around a buttoned boot as mute evidence of her tumble with Edwin.

As the fire merrily hissed and crackled, flames dancing high, Sophronia perched herself next to Lettice and speedily divested the young lady of all her clothes, piling them on the sofa next to her. Then she dropped to her knees at Lettice's feet, slipped her panties over and off their host foot and unbuttoned and removed her boots.

Jeremy, meanwhile, had rewound the gramophone. He selected some Bach harpsichord music. As it began to play, he looked into the fireside area and saw that Sophronia had stood up and was beginning to undo the pearl buttons of her bodice. 'I don't believe that I asked you to undress yourself,' he said, a sharp edge to his voice. Going to her, he took her hands off the buttons. 'Time enough for you to be nude in a while.'

Sophronia, visited by a genuine touch of annoyance, grimaced. Surrounded by naked flesh she was craving to be undressed herself – besides which, her now extremely needful pussy was giving her little peace. Nevertheless, she played along with their game. She found the champagne bottle, filled her glass and gulped from it.

Accustomed to his friend's sexual orchestrations and content to let him dictate the course of the evening's pleasure, Edwin parked his bare buttocks comfortably on the arm of a sofa, close to the fire, his cock at half-mast. Jeremy's eye flickered over his genitals. 'We might perhaps compromise though, Sophronia,' he said, getting on his knees by his wife's side. He glanced at Millie. 'Why don't you treat Edwin to a gobble, young lady?' he asked her. 'Meanwhile, I'll assist my wife out of just one important item of clothing.'

Pleased to take her cue, Millie knelt in front of Edwin and flattened her hands on his thighs, her fingers almost buried in his hair. As she ducked her head, lifted the tip of his fast rising prick with her tongue, and closed her mouth over it, Jeremy raised

55

the hem of Sophronia's skirt high and ducked beneath it, losing his head and back under the copious velveteen.

It was at that moment that Lord Brexford began to lose his iron control. His fingers trembled. Slipping his hands under the back of his wife's silken cami-knickers, he clutched her buttocks and moved her around until his cheeks nestled amidst the warm, soft flesh of her slightly parted upper thighs; he could just make out the glow of the fire through her dress. Reversing his hands, he hooked his fingers over the elasticated waistband of the knickers and dragged them down, turning them inside out until they rested on her thighs, covering his face. After indulging in a lengthy, luxurious sniff, he closed Sophronia's knees and slid the drawers down over them, and off. His nervous hands, betraying a rapidly building inner tension, sped back to her bare behind which he grabbed with fervent passion. As the tips of his pinkies met at Sophronia's anus, he poked out his tongue and pulled her loins to his mouth, lapping her pussy the way a cat laps at a saucer of milk.

Millie's fellatio was nothing less than enthusiastic, and as Sophronia lecherously watched her bobbing head whilst Jeremy's tongue probed her own vagina, she gasped loudly, spreading her knees wide, her hips twitching, her hands clenched at the back of his head where it humped her skirt. But sexual relief for her was not to be quite yet; there was still time for further, wickedly sweet, enforced frustration. If only her husband's tongue had fulfilled its initial promise she would have come most rapidly. But just as she was almost there it let her down. Unmouthing her and flinging her skirt over his head to free himself, he called for Edwin, with a slight shake in his voice.

'Why don't you give my wife a cock teasing?' he suggested.

Edwin, his cock deep in Millie's mouth, produced a raunchy, sloppy grin. Knowing exactly what Jeremy meant by this, and also aware of the house limitations as to what may or may not be done to its mistress, he was eager to comply. He lifted Millie's head off of his hard-on, rolled off the arm of the sofa to his feet and padded to Sophronia. Jeremy pulled up the front of her skirt and, bunch it high on her waist just beneath her bosom to expose her to the navel. 'Hold it like that,' he told her, as Edwin's eyes lustily latched on to a pussy wet with Jeremy's spittle.

Sophronia's smoky, begging gaze was riveted on Edwin's full, fat cock as he gripped it between two fingers and thumb and commenced to rub its fine, purple glans over her firm, white belly. Circling it in on her cute little indented navel, he poked it there as if attempting to fuck it – but he touched her with no other part of himself.

'You may take hold of his bollocks,' Lord Brexford said thickly, an order rather than a permission. As Sophronia did so, squeezing, Edwin trailed his cockhead down the almost invisible line of blonde hairs on her belly and into her pussy thatch. Bending slightly at the knees he worked his prick lower, sliding its full length beneath her crotch.

Edwin began to move his hips rhythmically. The solid back of his penis, cushioned in Sophronia's vulva, rocked between her fleshy lips. Jeremy stooped by her side to take hold of the hem at the back of her dress and to raise it high so that she could feel the fire's heat caressing her naked buttocks.

'Lettice, Millie,' said Jeremy urgently, 'come here, please.' As they joined the little group, he rasped, 'On

57

your knees Lettice, there's a good girl. Lick my wife's bum, do. As for you Millie, you may kiss her, play with her tits – do with her whatever comes into your head.'

With Lettice's tongue tracing a moist path up and down the crack of her bottom, unshy of its tiny hole, whilst Millie, at the same time, thrust her tongue deep in her ear and her hand down her bodice to tweak a nipple, Edwin's thick pole hotly, damply encased itself in her upper thighs and pussy lips and made thrusting, fucking motions, his balls hot in her palm. Sophronia became so weak she feared she was about to faint. Her hand let go of her dress which dropped to hang down on either side of Edwin's genitals, her arm flopped around his neck, and her weight sagged onto him.

At last Sophronia was blessed with the relief her body had craved for so long. As Lettice spread her buttocks and wormed her tongue into her bottom hole, as Millie's lewd attentions heated up and as Edwin's cock pounded away towards climax exactly as if it were inside her cunt, Sophronia squealed into Millie's mouth. Her entire body, so weak and limp seconds before, went rigid as she was seized with an orgasm so powerful it threatened to rip her apart.

Edwin erupted at almost the same moment, banging his cock hard between her thighs as his semen shot all over Lettice's neck to run and drip over her wobbling breasts.

Sophronia caved in on herself. She slid down Edwin with his weight leaning on her. As she did so, the author's still unflagging erection jumped from under the skirt hem to trail up the fabric. Sophronia ended up on her knees with her cheek flattened against his strong, hairy belly as his cock, leaking slightly, came to rest on her shoulder.

All this while Jeremy had been masturbating at his contrived scene. Now, eyes wantonly drooping, hand almost still on his throbbing shaft, he sat astride the arm of a sofa. Voice heavy with lust he muttered, 'If you now bring Sophronia to me, Lettice, I shall show you all what a peer of the realm fancies doing at this moment to his lady. I trust you got her arsehole good and wet with your tongue?'

Lettice, not without difficulty, coaxed Sophronia to her feet. With an arm around her back and a hand beneath her armpit she walked her, Sophronia's knees wobbling, to Jeremy, as Edwin sunk into a squat on the rug, glazed eyes fixed on the fire. Millie, considerably aroused by all this dissolution, took her own initiative by sitting below Jeremy in a corner of the sofa and reaching up, cradled his balls.

'Oh, but yes,' grunted Jeremy, enclosing her hand with his own to bring it up so that it held both balls and cockshaft, 'you may most certainly assist in the buggery.' His gaze swept goatishly over his wife who, still partially supported by Lettice, was recovering from her orgasm as her head began to pound with thoughts of what was to befall her next.

'The dress, I fear, will be an encumbrance.' Jeremy brought Millie's hand up his cock and back to his balls as he said, 'You may now be nude, madam – but keep your shoes on, do.' He paused. 'See to it, why don't you, Lettice?'

Nimble fingers unfastened Sophronia's bodice and waistband. Eager to have Lady Brexford's charms fully revealed to her, Lettice pulled the shoulders and sleeves down to her elbows and then swiftly stripped the dress off. Sophronia, who had been wearing no undergarment other than her camiknickers, was naked beneath it.

Jeremy's eyes lasciviously gleamed, his hands once again exhibited a slight tremble. 'Open her cheeks and position her bottom,' he told Lettice with shaky voice. 'And you, Millie, put plenty of spit on my dick, why don't you?'

In itself however, Millie's saliva proved to be an insufficient lubricant. Having applied it orally, she directed the wet glans at Sophronia's little, puckered hole as Lettice lowered Lady Brexford's bottom onto it. But as the ribald penetration began, as Jeremy's cockhead started to vanish into the stretched, pink place, Sophronia let forth a howl of pain; anal sex, though infinitely pleasing to her, was a relatively new delight to which her sphincter was far from accustomed.

Concerned, Jeremy's efforts ceased and he at once withdrew. 'Hell, that truly hurt,' gasped Sophronia. 'Don't try it again without jelly, please?'

'Edwin?' Jeremy grunted. His friend remained squatting, staring blankly into the flames. 'I say, Edwin?'

Blinking himself back into reality, Edwin turned around. 'What is it?'

'You know where I keep the petroleum jelly, do you not?'

Edwin now noticed the lewd position into which Sophronia had been manoeuvred, and realised that the others all had their part to play in her prospective sodomisation as, indeed, had he. Clambering to his feet, he went to a cabinet and brought from it a tin of the jelly, working off the lid as he approached the grossly expectant group. Lettice's hands remained poised on Sophronia's buttocks, keeping them spread, as Millie teased her bottom hole with the head of Jeremy's cock, rubbing it back and forth.

'Good. Stick some up her arsehole, Edwin,' muttered Jeremy. 'And you grease my pole Millie.'

Lettice opened Sophronia's anus as wide as it would go and the cold jelly was thrust into it by Edwin's fingers, which twisted and turned in priapic enthusiasm. Sophronia luxuriously shivered. With a long and noisy intake of breath she closed her eyes, feeling thoroughly besmirched and splendidly wicked.

Driven to a new peak of salaciousness by Millie's hand slipping and sliding on his hard-on, and at the sight of Edwin finger-poking his wife's bottom hole which was framed and stretched by vermilion-tipped fingers, Jeremy could wait no longer. 'Give me her bum now. Give it to me,' he gasped.

Edwin's attentions ceased and Lettice lowered Sophronia's buttocks as Millie guided his lordship's cockhead. Sophronia's eyes jumped open as she emitted a low howl, but this time one of pain and pleasure in equal amounts; her sphincter gave in without too much fuss and she sank down, aided by Lettice, onto her husband's prick.

The moments of hurt quickly passed, and there remained only the incredibly lewd and horny sensation of having her backside thoroughly stuffed. As Jeremy, his movements restricted by his position and Sophronia's weight, jerked his buttocks against the sofa arm, Sophronia began to bounce lustily. Her eyes closed tight once more as she chewed the inside of her bottom lip.

Lord and Lady Brexford found a mutually pleasing bum-balling rhythm as the other three greedily watched the hearty buggery. He leaned into the end of the back of the sofa, his hands spread over and supporting her bottom, as her tits and the single string of pearls resting on them jiggled and trembled.

Jeremy's entire face was distorted with bawdiness as he feasted on the sight of his cock steadily disappearing into and reappearing from his wife's tight hole.

Sophronia knew from her limited experience that she would not reach orgasm by anal sex alone. Reaching between her legs she shoved two fingers inside her moist pussy and found the hard nub of her clitoris with the ball of her thumb. She began to masturbate at double the speed that her bottom bounced.

Edwin had sunk down into the sofa with the other two women on either side of him, his arms around their shoulders and his hands loose on their tits, fingers playing with their nipples. Lettice's palm was wrapped around his prick, slowly helping it on its way up again, and Millie was cupping his balls, but all three were at that moment more intent on the buggery, becoming more fervent by the second, than on pleasuring one another.

For the second time that evening the often long-staying Jeremy failed to contain himself – not that he entertained any pressing ambition in that direction. Seldom was he driven to greater heights of lust than by a bum-fuck, and tonight's event was proving exceptionally racy. Orgasm took an irrevocable hold of him. He stilled Sophronia's buttocks, his prick tightly, warmly, buried all the way up between them, and the floodgates opened.

Feeling Jeremy's thigh muscles go tense and solid beneath her, his fingers digging almost cruelly into her backside, Sophronia began to pant as her frigging reached its wildest. With hot sperm shooting into her to bring to her bowels a sensation of unparalleled raunchiness, she let forth a strangled scream. Her climactic juices seeped over her fingers which, apart from a tremble in their tips, had now stilled within her.

Sophronia remained sitting, fully impaled and motionless, on Jeremy's softening cock for long seconds, as the effects of their mutually exhausting, rewarding orgasms surged through them both. Then she slowly rolled sideways off her husband's thighs and his damp and greasy pole, to collapse across the three naked laps on the sofa.

Edwin's fully erect cock invaded the softness of her belly.

Chapter Six

Having partaken of a rollickingly debauched week-end and having slept off his excesses through Monday morning, Lord Brexford enjoyed a roast beef salad lunch washed down with a crisp Riesling wine before setting off, alone, to exercise himself and his favourite steed.

Mounted on Napoleon, a pure-bred Arab stallion of sixteen hands, Jeremy cantered smartly around the well-worn, slightly soggy bridle-paths in his woods, savouring the freshness of a clear-skied autumn after-noon and the exuberance of the horse, feeling in the very pink of health. There was no thought of sex in his mind until he slowed down to a trot and left his private grounds for the public domain. Perceiving in the distance Chalmers Finishing School for Young Ladies, its whitewashed walls glinting in the sunlight, he reined in the panting, sweaty Napoleon. Standing tall in the stirrups he let his eyes wander over the school and grounds. Too far away to be distinguished clearly as individuals, a number of girls were playing hockey, calf-length skirts swirling around their long socks. Indistinct figures they may have been, but this did not prevent Jeremy's prurient brain from getting busy; within a moment's canter from him were twenty-two girls, perhaps virgins all, aged between seventeen and nineteen, dashing energetically about, their tits bouncing, their bottoms trembling – amongst them no doubt the one he had observed getting her bare backside caned just three nights before.

With a heavy sigh of desire, mind once again crowded with the lubricious thoughts never out of it for long, Jeremy sat back in the saddle and began to walk his horse alongside the boundary fence of Chalmers, wondering, as he had so often before, how he might get access to one or two of those so carefully chaperoned young ladies. As the hockey field became hidden from his view by a little copse, he turned away from the fence and began to trot along a winding, rutted, hedge-lined country lane.

Rounding a bend he saw, ahead of him, on the crest of a small slope, a pony and trap approaching. It got rapidly closer, harness tinkling and when it had almost reached him, Jeremy noticed two interesting facts at much the same time; its sole occupant, the driver, was the chubby headmistress of Chalmers, Miss Petty – and one of its two, huge, steel-rimmed wooden wheels appeared to be loose. The wheel was wobbling precariously from side to side, a fact to which Miss Petty seemed oblivious.

'Your wheel – look to your wheel!' Jeremy called out as the rig trundled past him.

However Miss Petty, face slightly flushed as she cracked her whip above the trotting pony's flanks, did not quite catch the implication of his words. 'What?' she shouted, turning her head.

This was the moment when a cotter-pin worked its way out of the wheel-hub, and a second security pin snapped. The wheel rolled away. The trap, beginning to negotiate a bend ahead of it, tilted on its remaining wheel, stayed upright for a second then, as the bend straightened, it slowly keeled over to deposit its custodian, skirt and petticoat flying high as she screamed, in the hawthorn hedge. The pony continued to drag the stricken cart for a hundred yards or so along the lane, then stopped.

Turning Napoleon around, Jeremy hurried to the scene. Miss Petty was in a most undignified position, face down across the hedge, crushed into it, her white lace bloomers on display. She was trying to free herself, but had no purchase since her feet were off the ground. Dismounting, eyes naturally searching out the woman's underwear, Jeremy put his strong hands around her waist and helped her out of her predicament.

Miss Petty nervously straightened her hat and smoothed down her dress. She had a slight scratch on her cheek, but she was wearing gloves, so that her hands were unlacerated.

'Are you all right?' Jeremy asked.

'I, I think so,' she said, picking up a fallen shoe and slipping it back on. She stared in annoyance past where the wheel had come to rest against the hedge, to the distressed pony, which was dragging the broken trap around in small circles. 'What an incredibly stupid thing to happen.'

'Well, it could have been far worse. You might easily have broken a bone.' Jeremy took hold of his horse's reins and patted its neck.

'Yes, I might have indeed. Thank you for your help.' She extended a hand. 'I am Miss Claire Petty.'

'And I Lord Brexford, at your service, madam.' He shook the hand warmly, realising that this chance encounter might turn out to be fortuitous.

Miss Petty's face exhibited surprise. 'Lord . . .?' she said. 'Oh. From the manor, then? I'm delighted to meet you, Your Lordship.'

'Deal Manor, yes.' He artfully appraised her. 'But am I not somehow familiar with your name, Miss Petty?'

'That's possible. I'm headmistress of Chalmers.'

'The finishing school? I see.' Thinking quickly, Jeremy glanced down the lane. He decided to take charge of the situation. 'Well, first we must free your pony,' he said briskly, 'then we'll see about getting you back to the school. No doubt you are suffering some mild form of shock.'

Leaving Napoleon's reins in Miss Petty's hands, Jeremy went to the pony and unharnessed him, brain scheming as to how he could turn this event to his advantage. Going back to his horse, he mounted and persuaded Miss Petty to climb up sidesaddle in front of him. In this fashion, the pony meekly tagging along behind, he took her back to Chalmers.

By the time they reached the front doors of the finishing school, Lord Brexford had conceived of a plan. The hockey game had just come to an end and he unobtrusively examined the girls who filed curiously past on their way into the building, as the headmistress dismounted. He was rewarded with a glimpse of Ellie Branks, which spurred on his determination.

'I cannot thank you enough, My Lord,' said Miss Petty.

'Oddly enough, it has just occurred to me how you may return the favour,' he told her.

'Well, of course. Anything.'

He took a deep breath, letting it out slowly as his eyes wandered over her face before launching his idea. Then he said, 'As headmistress of this establishment, no doubt you are fully trained in the art of castigation?'

She appeared most startled, blinking rapidly. 'I am,

67

naturally – but is that not a rather extraordinary question, with respect?'

'I suppose it could be considered so, yes. But not under the circumstances. You see we – that is Lady Brexford and I – have a parlour maid who has regrettably taken to petty pilfering lately. She's been caught bang to rights, but we're not keen, as would normally be the case, to let her go because she happens to be rather good at her work. She needs to be punished, of course.'

As he paused, staring at her, Miss Petty began, 'I'm not sure if . . .' but he cut in.

'It would be most unsuitable for my wife or myself to administer a beating, and unthinkable for any of the staff to do so. I thought that perhaps you, in the light of your general position of authority over young wenches, would be kind enough to do the necessary?'

'Well, I really don't . . .'

'Come now, Miss Petty,' interrupted Jeremy again, jovially, 'did you just not state you would do anything to return my favour?'

'Indeed. But . . .'

'Then that settles the matter.' He made an elaborate show of consulting his fob watch. 'My chauffeur will pick you up at, let us say . . . seven, tomorrow evening? How does that suit you?'

Flustered, but not a little intrigued by Lord Brexford's remarkable request, Miss Petty seemed to be left with no option but to agree.

Meg Willard, downstairs maid, had not the slightest idea how a handsome pair of Georgian silver candlesticks which went missing from the drawing room that evening came to be discovered at the back of a drawer in her room by the butler the following morning. That someone had hidden them there to make her appear guilty of a crime seemed clear, but who or why she had no idea. Hauled before His Lordship, trembling and ashen, she stammered out her innocence, but it soon became obvious to her that in no way was she going to be believed. She was not, she was informed to her relief, to be fired; appropriately severe punishment would be pronounced on her early in the evening after Lord Brexford had had time to consider what form it should take.

Meg imagined that she was to be given extra, heavy duties, or that her wages were to be cut for a period of time – both of which prospects filled her with dismay. But confronted at seven-thirty in his study by Lord Brexford and a stern-looking woman she had never seen before, and informed that she was to be thrashed, she rebelled; a proud lass, she would rather be given the sack than submit to such a painful indignity, and she boldly made this known.

'Dismissed you may also be, if you so wish, but a beating you richly deserve in any case, and therefore a beating shall you suffer,' Jeremy informed her blandly.

Her rather handsome, dimpled chin rose in defiance as a blush coloured Meg's cheeks. 'No Your Lordship. No, not I,' she told him, and made for the door. He swooped past her, reaching it first, locked it and slipped the key in his pocket.

'You are going nowhere until you have been punished, my girl,' said Jeremy. 'I advise you to submit quietly and afterwards return to your duties, and no more will be said about the matter.'

Meg's troubled eyes flickered from her master to the silently waiting Miss Petty, and back again. 'But I didn't steal them candlesticks, I really didn't,' she protested.

'It is futile to add lying to your transgression.' Jeremy unbuckled his heavy leather belt. 'You will kindly bend over my desk, young lady.'

Her blush turned scarlet. She backed away. 'With respect, My Lord, I shall do no such thing,' she said.

'But I order it.' He doubled over his belt and handed it to Miss Petty. Taking it, Claire experienced a stirring of excitement at the solid feel of it in her hand. Her eye dwelt speculatively on her intended victim, a girl of no more than twenty, in her way quite pretty, and with hips shapely and enticing beneath a black cotton dress which fell to her ankles.

Rushing to the door, Meg rattled its knob uselessly, insisting noisily that she be let out. Despite her agitated state, there was a great deal of spirit in her. She said, with remarkable resolution, 'I'll take none of your orders no more, sir, because I'm leavin' this 'ouse right away.'

'Do you then oblige me to use force?'

'You ain't got the right.'

'Have I not? We shall see about that. Now, you will kindly prostrate yourself across my desk this instant.'

'I won't.'

'Very well.' Jeremy dived for her, grabbed her by the wrist and dragged the maid to his elegant, spindly French desk. She screamed protest and struggled valiantly, but her shouts fell on unheeding ears and she was no match for the wirily powerful Lord Brexford. 'Please help me, Miss Petty,' he panted, moving to the other end of the desk from Meg, whilst leaning across it to keep firm hold of her wrist as he undid his cravat and held it out to the headmistress.

A half-minute later, one of Meg's hands was firmly attached to the top of a thin desk leg. As she continued to struggle and to shout protests, Jeremy searched the room with his eyes for something else convenient with which to bind her. They fell on a silken, thin, tasselled rope holding a curtain bunched in the middle, then jumped to its companion. In the space of another minute the curtains were hanging loose and Meg found herself secured lengthways across the desk, both hands and one ankle tied to its legs. There was little need to attach her free ankle; Meg was well and truly married to the desk top. Tears of anger and frustration welled in her eyes. She fell silent.

Jeremy was breathing a touch heavily from his exertions. As he stood back to survey the trussed maid, Claire Petty noted a faint gleam in his eyes which she rightly interpreted as indicating rather more than satisfaction at the justice that was about to be meted out. For a second, as he glanced with the hint of a smile, from Meg to her, a silent message of mutal understanding passed between them. Pursing her lips, Claire picked up the belt from where she had left it draped over a chair back and doubled it over, to grip it firmly by the buckle and its opposite end.

'I imagine you would usually make use of a cane?' asked Jeremy.

Miss Petty slapped the heavy belt across her palm to test it. 'This will do very nicely,' she said, surveying the buxom behind which was to be her target.

'Then lay it on thick and heavy – the girl needs to be doubly punished for her insolence in refusing to cooperate.'

The headmistress licked her lips. 'Now?'

'Yes, now.'

There was a sob from Meg at the words; her buttocks perceptibly clenched beneath their black cotton covering. However, she could not hear Jeremy's next words which he whispered in Miss Petty's ear. 'In fact, do not hurt her too much,' he said, to her surprise. 'Sting her, that's all.'

Wondering anew at the Lord's motivation, a little disappointed even, Miss Petty lifted her belt hand, measured her distance and lashed with curtailed force across Meg's taut backside. The belt connected with a muffled thump, accompanied by a shriek – more of shock than of pain – from the hapless Meg, whose free foot convulsed behind her to throw off its soft, flat shoe. A brief pause and Miss Petty brought the belt down twice more, each blow punctuated by a somewhat unnecessary yelp from Meg. Then Jeremy stayed her hand.

'I have heard,' muttered Lord Brexford, his gaze piercing the maid's skirt, 'that on occasion, before being beaten, errant young ladies have been known to tuck an exercise book or some such thing into their drawers in order to absorb some of the pain of a flogging. How can we be sure that . . .?'

As she answered his unspoken thought, Claire Petty noted a smouldering in his eye which seemed to be in tune with her libido. 'Of course, there is only one way,' she said.

'Quite. Naturally, one hesitates to be considered prurient. However . . .' He nodded towards Meg's haunches. 'An inspection is in order, I do believe.'

'Yes. Indeed one has to be sure.'

Slowly, Miss Petty hitched the maid's skirt all the way up the backs of long, white legs, which were bare except for short, black ankle socks, and draped the fabric over the small of her back to expose white, cambric camiknickers. She flattened a hand on each of Meg's buttocks in turn, swallowing back her excitement as she felt the warmth of them through the material. 'She certainly appears to be uncushioned,' she told Jeremy.

Sure of his ground with Miss Petty – surer than she could know – he reached for Meg's bottom. As he said, 'But let us be absolutely certain,' at Meg's wail of protest and shame, he hooked his fingers into the waistband of her knickers and dragged them down until they rested beneath fully exposed, plumpish buttocks. 'Ahhh,' he pronounced, 'quite unprotected, then.'

Miss Petty caught her breath. She felt her pussy beginning to dampen as she responded, delightfully going along with what she now realised was nothing more than an elaborate, harmless sex game, and perhaps should stay that way?

'My dear Miss Petty,' he murmured, eyes laughing wickedly into hers, 'I must congratulate you. You certainly seem to understand the finer points of a good and proper drubbing.'

'Shall I proceed?'

'But most definitely. And spare her not.' But he winked.

'If I may just ...' the headmistress eased Meg's knickers further down her spread thighs, 'increase the target area?'

'Please do. An excellent notion.' Jeremy's eyes lustily probed. Nicely exposed now, rudely framed between fleshy thigh tops and taut knicker waistband, was a hefty tuft of curly, auburn-tinted pubic hair. He resisted the sudden urge to do with his fingers to that tempting area what his gaze had already done, and grinned slackly as cowhide connected with unprotected female rump with a sound like a soft handclap, to leave a slight smudge of redness.

Claire Petty looked up for a reaction from Lord

73

Brexford after each slap. Understanding that this so-called punishment was nothing more than an excuse for lickerishness on his part, and wondering at the deviousness of a mind that could have contrived to get her to the manor to administer it, she needed to be sure she was not beginning to hit too hard. Nevertheless, she laid into Meg's quivering buttocks with a certain amount of enthusiasm, encouraged by her moist pussy which twitched and throbbed with every blow.

The belt was certainly stinging Meg; her buttocks were turning pink and very warm and her tears flowed freely, splashing down onto the Persian rug beneath her face. The tears were not of pain, rather of helpless embarrassment at her humiliation.

More than thirty times the belt rose and fell to the mutually intense pleasure of both Claire Petty and Lord Brexford. When Jeremy, cock straining and tenting his trousers, called a halt, Meg's backside was an undamaged, but healthily rosy blotch.

Miss Petty's arms went loose at her sides, the belt trailing on the rug as she watched Jeremy hoist the girl's knickers back into place. She did not fail to notice how the palms of his hands caressed the hot buttocks, and the tips of two fingers trailed over Meg's pussy as he performed this operation. He let her skirt drop to the floor with obvious regret, then quickly freed her.

Meg, tears still rolling down her cheeks, was cramped; Lord Brexford was obliged to assist her to her feet. He walked her, by her elbow, to the door and unlocked it. He let her out without either of them saying a word and then, causing Miss Petty's eyebrows to rise, he relocked the door.

He stared silently at the headmistress for long

moments, a twisted smile on his face, eyes wandering over her, seeming to peer through her clothes. Then he said, 'I shall take the liberty of divining your feelings at this moment, my dear Miss Petty.'

She stared steadily back, amused, intrigued, raunchy – and almost consumed by the usual need for sexual relief after having administered punishment. 'Please do,' she invited him.

He moved very close to her so that his breath, smelling not unpleasantly of vintage port and Havana cigars, brushed her face as he spoke. 'I venture to suggest that you are a woman who takes perverted pleasure out of thrashing bare behinds. That your most cherished possession is the cane which hangs over the fireplace in your study.'

Miss Petty gasped. 'How can you possibly . . .?'

'That you are somewhat of a sadist, and that you achieve a peak of sexual excitement from the administration of pain.' He thrust his face even closer to hers so that their noses bumped. In a highly aroused condition himself, he had no reservations about pushing his point firmly home. 'Your fanny, dear lady, is of course most wet at this moment. Your normal course of action, having dismissed your victim, would be to raise your skirts and to frig yourself to orgasm.' His eyes drilled into hers. 'Is that not so?'

'I . . . I . . . what are you saying, sir?'

'That this . . .' he jammed his hand between her legs to clutch fiercely at her crotch through her maroon satin skirt, 'is in urgent need of relief.'

Going rubbery at the knees, she made a feeble attempt to brush his hand away for some reason. Then she gave in, closing her thighs on it and gasping as he squeezed. The tips of his strong fingers dug and jiggled. 'Most urgent, I'd say,' he murmured. His lips closed in on her ear. 'As is my dick, dear lady.'

Taking her hand, he placed it flat over the bulge in his trousers. 'We must join these two needy parts of our anatomies without delay.'

Claire Petty, overcome with a sexual craving so powerful that all her inhibitions fell away, got suddenly very dirty. Moaning, 'Oh yes, My Lord, we two must fuck,' she fumbled clumsily with his fly buttons, and tearing them open, shoved her hand inside, ripped apart his underpants buttons and dragged his sturdy cock into the light. 'Fuck me, fuck me, stick this monster up my cunt,' she mumbled, driving herself to further heights of salaciousness by her crude language, as she greedily groped cock and balls.

Using both hands, he shoved her away from him and spun her around. 'Over my desk, just like Meg,' he rasped.

'God, oh God yes.' She flattened herself on the fancy green leather top with an utterly unseemly eagerness. 'Are you going to tie me up? Will you, will you thrash me?'

'Aha. A masochist as well as a sadist have I found. A fitting combination,' he grunted. Taking her skirt by its hem, he swept it up into a crumpled heap around her hips. His hands roved over the tightly stretched knickers, his fingers slipping under their elastic, and with one determined heave he had them hanging about her knees. 'But I shan't beat you on this occasion.' He leaned into her, glans teasing the crack of her bottom. 'To quote your own words, I shall stick this monster up your cunt.' Roughly grasping her buttocks, with his fingertips on either side of her vulva, he spread her pussy lips wide and thrust his cock deep inside her. As he banged it all the way in, up to his balls, he muttered, 'But I fancy when I do get around to flogging you, you will not be spared as we spared Meg!'

The combined effect of Claire Petty's softly plump, white and slightly frecked behind, twin shuddering cushions for Jeremy's heaving loins, and her wonderfully slippery vagina which was surprisingly tight for a woman of her age, caused Jeremy to rut like a rampant bull. The desk shook and creaked under his violent assault, occasionally shifting on the rug as he rammed his cock home.

Having been unserved by male flesh for well over a month, and already brought to the brink of climax by her strapping of Meg, Miss Petty went very quickly and gratefully over the top. She began to gasp and whimper her way through a string of orgasms as her feverish, soaking pussy clenched and unclenched on Jeremy's cock like the hand of a milkmaid on the udder of a cow. To further stoke the fires of her sexual delirium, with each hefty plunge on his shaft Jeremy partially granted her request for a thrashing by heavily slapping first one buttock, then the other, with resounding, hurtful blows which made them tremble and left smudges of reddening evidence of his potency stark against the whiteness of her skin.

Had Jeremy been able to sustain this strenuous and sadistic screw for ever Claire would surely have remained happily prostrated across his desk for all eternity, with her pussy and buttocks begging for more. But, inevitable under the circumstances, his staying power was limited to some fifteen minutes after which his testicles, crushed into the edge of the desk, erupted forth their copious load of semen, causing the recipient such pleasure that as her pussy was flooded, she came with a shout so loud it caused a window to rattle.

Lord Brexford remained flattened against Miss Petty's back for almost a minute, his penis shrinking within her despite the fact that her vagina continued to go through tiny contractions. Then he slipped out of her to sink down to his knees on the rug, hands on buttocks turned fiery from his slapping, nose inches from a pussy out of which his semen trickled. He studied the object of his violent copulation with a sated yet still prurient eye. He opened its soft lips. He eased two fingers into the wetness as Claire Petty eagerly, expectantly, awaited his next move. But finally, to her keen disappointment, Claire felt her knickers being hoisted into place and then her skirt was lowered over the backs of her legs.

Getting to his feet, Jeremy put away his flaccid cock, buttoned himself up, took the headmistress of Chalmers by the elbow and helped her off the desk. Going to the coal fire, he replenished and stoked it, coaxing it into bright flames then, as she watched him, and finding nothing to say, he half-filled two glasses with brandy, took one over and gave it her. Casually, he told her, 'Sit down, do, Claire. You and I must have a serious discussion – about sex.'

Sipping from her glass, she sank into an armchair near the fire, comfortably aware of her wet, contented pussy. She stared at him in a slightly dazed fashion, still hardly able to believe what had occurred between them, as he leaned an arm on the heavy, wooden mantelpiece. 'Oh. We must?' she responded weakly.

'But most definitely. I find in you a woman of somewhat unusual tastes in that direction. For instance, you enjoy a frantic frigging after soundly caning your charges. You . . .'

'How on earth do you . . .?' Miss Petty interrupted, only to have her words cut off in turn.

'I shall come to that. As has just been demon-
strably, conclusively proved, you are most partial to
a thorough swiving – surrounded by females as you
are, I doubt the opportunity to indulge comes often
enough for you. I venture to suggest that . . .' He
paused to take a cigar from the humidor on the mantelpiece, perusing her with piercing but amused eyes
as he sliced off its end. '. . . your cravings go even
further beyond the tastes I have mentioned. That you
are possessed of a most versatile and exotic mind in
certain forbidden directions. No?' He thrust a
wooden spill into the flames and lit his cigar with it,
his eyes flickering from its end to Miss Petty and back
again as he did so. 'No?'

'Really, sir. Really. Are you not being over-bold?'

'And have you not just been so?' The words bit
through a cloud of smoke.

'The heat of the moment.'

'As hot as my fire – as I am convinced you are,
Claire. Now, I myself – and I confess this since I
believe we may be mutually useful to one another –
am addicted to certain sexual practices which many
would describe as bizarre. For instance, I throw regular, intimate parties here in the manor. Let me describe them more bluntly as orgies which frequently
lean towards the sado-masochistic.' He puffed on the
cigar, his gaze eating into her. 'I'd bet my best pair of
riding boots that you would give your thrashing arm
to attend one now and again.'

Miss Petty's mind began to race in previously un-
dared directions as she realised that the door to a
dark, sexual world undreamed of was being opened
for her. But she said, 'You presume too much.'

'Do I?' Jeremy decided that this was the moment
for full confession. 'About my certain knowledge of

you which so puzzled you? I recently acquired a most powerful telescope through which I am able to obtain an admirable view of your study.' He mouthed a flat smile. 'Who is the lovely blonde creature with the diamond-shaped mole on her buttock?'

Swallowing brandy so fast it burnt her throat and made her splutter, Miss Petty stammered, 'You dare to . . .?'

'Having cruelly flogged that delicious bottom and sent the poor young girl on her way, you treated yourself to a good frigging. So you see, I really do know quite a lot about you.' He dipped the end of his cigar in his brandy, smelt it and took a quiet puff. Then he said compellingly, as she poured more fire into her churning belly, 'And now of course I have rogered you and therefore know rather more.'

Being normally a very light drinker, it took but a few more seconds for the effects of the strong spirit to reach Miss Petty's head. Her indignation went into retreat; the liquor greatly emboldened her. 'And I now know something of you.'

'Indeed you do. But only the smallest fraction.'

Raising an eyebrow, she stared pointedly at his trouser front. 'Hardly small, My Lord.'

He laughed. 'That's better. I believe we begin to understand one another.'

'What is it exactly you want of me?'

'It's really very simple. I have a yearning, an almost intolerable craving, to sample some of the virgin flesh under your authority. Young, protected, nubile females of good class and breeding are amongst the most desirable creatures on earth. There must be more than a hundred of them at Chalmers – but a stone's throw from here. If you could somehow contrive, now and then, to get one of the more juicy of them up here your rewards would be . . .' he left the fireplace with both brandy glass and cigar in the same hand, and fondled her breasts with the other, 'considerable.'

'Considerable, perhaps, but hardly to be presented in Heaven,' muttered the headmistress, half to herself. But a shiver of delight ran through her. She clasped his breast-marauding hand and squeezed her thighs together. She needed to speak slowly to avoid slurring her words. 'Sado-masochism, you mentioned. Beatings and so forth?'

'To which I would like to add the occasional deflowering.'

Unwisely, Miss Petty drained her glass, mind racing. 'That gel you mentioned? The one with the pretty mole? Ellie Branks is her name. A most libidinous wench, as it turns out. I discovered afterwards that she actually took pleasure from her thrashing.' She told him about Ellie and Georgina, and what she had overheard.

Jeremy's eyes positively shone. 'Then we must devise a scheme whereby Ellie will be invited to the manor. You will make the invitation on my behalf – and she must come alone.' His hand found its way inside Claire's bodice to grab a nipple which he pinched and twisted. 'Then you are prepared to cooperate fully?'

Her vision went momentarily fuzzy. Her head spun. She gasped as he tweaked her nipple almost viciously. 'I'll get Ellie for you, so I shall.'

'Good. Oh, excellent.' Jeremy found himself once again mightily aroused, this time by thoughts of what he might do to Ellie when he had her in his clutches. 'Get her here as soon as possible, perhaps tomorrow evening, and I guarantee to make you the star of next

81

weekend's little orgy. In the meantime . . .' he carefully placed his brandy glass on a side table and, with his cigar clamped between his teeth unbuttoned his trousers to fish out his swollen, almost fully erect penis, 'we might perhaps seal our pact not with blood, but with sperm.' Closing in on Miss Petty, he rubbed his glans on her cheek. 'Will you not gamahuche me?'

For a moment, as she wetted her lips, Claire saw two cocks. Choosing one, she tongued it deep into her mouth, avidly sucking.

Chapter Seven

As Ellie waited, dressed in her Sunday-best clothes, to be picked up and taken to Deal Manor, her mind was in somewhat of a turmoil. She had been instructed by Miss Petty to be in the hall near the front doors at five minutes to seven, and told that on no account was she to keep Lord and Lady Brexford waiting.

So there she was, alone – since the rest of the school was at supper – a little nervous and quite unsure why she, of all the girls, had been selected for what Petters had described as 'a most especially privileged evening'. All she had been told was that the Brexfords had expressed a desire to entertain one of Miss Petty's girls, and had left it up to her to select a suitable guest. They were, she had said, a most charming and noble couple who had had the notion that a young lady from Chalmers, of similar social standing to themselves, might benefit from escaping a school meal to dine at their table. Ellie had been chosen to be the first to enjoy this opportunity, a fact which remained a total mystery to her since she assumed she was still in the headmistress's bad books over the *Justine* affair.

The harsh honk of a klaxon startled her. Gathering her heavy cloak around her, she pulled its hood up over her head, opened the door apprehensively and stepped out into the blustery, drizzly darkness where an impressive example of the horseless carriage awaited her.

As she was let into the rear of the black limousine she realised that it was not empty. 'Good evening Miss Branks – or, rather, an inclement one,' said Jeremy Brexford, taking Ellie's kid-gloved hand as she settled next to him and the door was closed on them. 'I am Lord Brexford. I rather thought, in view of the unusual circumstances, that it would be a gesture of politeness to collect you in person.' His thin lips crinkled into a pleasant smile as his droopy brown eyes wandered appreciatively over her face.

A horde of butterflies seemed to Ellie to be flapping around in her stomach as the strong hand squeezed hers warmly. She caught the lord's eyes only briefly before lowering hers to her lap in confusion whilst muttering, 'Good, good evening sir.' As the car rolled off towards the gates, Jeremy's hand kept hold of Ellie's for longer than protocol demanded, but she was too flustered to notice. When he unclasped it, his eyes remained latched to her face.

'Well, Miss Petty has certainly sent us a very fine-looking young lady,' he commented. 'I must remember to congratulate her on her most excellent taste.' Ellie coloured slightly; she would have blushed scarlet to the soles of her feet had she known what Lord Brexford had in his mind at that moment: a vivid image of her bare bottom with its tantalising diamond-shaped mole.

Ellie produced a mumbled thank you, then pulled herself together to blurt out words she had prepared for use on her arrival at the manor. 'It was most kind of you to invite me, My Lord.'

'Common courtesy. We are neighbours – but I

could hardly invite the entire school so you are, shall we say, representing them.' He paused. 'If you don't mind, I shall call you by your first name. What is it?'

'Ellie.'

'Well, Ellie, you must call me Jeremy.'

'Jeremy.' She blinked. 'Yes.'

'We, er, we appreciate pretty girls very much up at the manor.' They had already reached his private wood, and the car's big lamps cut a bright swathe through the overhanging branches ahead.

'Oh.' Tongue-tied again, Ellie gazed out of her window into the dripping, somewhat eerie darkness.

'There's absolutely no need to be shy, you know.'

She started as he flattened his hand on her cheek and turned her face towards him. Hesitantly raising her eyes to his, she discovered it was so black in the car that she could hardly make out more than the outline of his face. Feeling somehow protected by the dimness, she managed a weak smile. 'I'm always a little shy at first when I meet someone new,' she said. 'I shall be quite all right in a while.'

'Ah. Good.' Jeremy dropped his hand from her face to the back of her gloved hand and patted it. 'Yes. I'm sure you'll be very all right.'

Deal Manor, ancient pile, presented itself as a huge and brooding shadow in the dark, wet night. With very few of its windows lit it looked positively ghostly.

But Ellie had little fear of ghosts. In any case, the building was a familiar if habitually distant sight and its sheer size failed to inspire awe since her own family home was equally large – a sprawling Victorian estate in Sussex. As, with squeaking brakes, the car pulled up near the front doors, she began to find her confidence and to wonder what the evening might have in store.

One of the double doors swung outwards, and a uniformed flunky appeared in the pool of light spilling from the hallway opening a brolly to escort firstly Ellie, and then his master, to the house.

Sophronia Brexford, wearing a stunning, peach lace evening gown cut low in front almost to the nipples, greeted them enthusiastically in the great hall. 'Why, you are lovely!' she exclaimed, as Ellie was relieved of her cloak and gloves.

'Her name is Ellie,' said Jeremy.

'You are most welcome, my dear.' Sophronia lightly kissed her on both cheeks. 'Rather a pretty name.'

'Thank you.' Sophronia's outgoing personality and charming appearance helped Ellie to relax further. 'It's from Heloise, actually.'

'Of course, the French. French names seem to be so popular these days, do they not? Mine is Sophronia.' Jeremy had introduced her only as 'my wife, Lady Brexford.'

'From the Greek.' She tittered gaily. 'It's supposed to mean I'm prudent and temperate.'

'Which I fear is far from the truth,' commented Jeremy as he escorted Ellie, his hand on the elbow of her long-sleeved, blue satin dress, Sophronia at her side, through the hall and into the drawing-room with its roaring, crackling fire. 'She is headstrong, and she sometimes imbibes a little more than is good for her – but then she is very young and full of spirit. I doubt if you yourself are all that much younger than her – how old are you, Ellie?'

'I'm eighteen and almost a half.'

He had her sit on a sofa, upon which many hearty sexual calisthenics had been indulged in and which flanked the fire. 'Sophronia's just twenty-two. There you are, you see, not much difference in fact between you, is there? And I just bet you are also a spirited wench.' Picking up a small silver bell from an oak table he rang it vigorously, its jangling echoing in the big room. 'What will you drink before supper?'

She thought about this as a butler silently appeared. 'We're not allowed alcohol at Chalmers. Lord . . . Jeremy.'

'But you're not at Chalmers now, are you?' He turned a dazzling smile on her, with a heavier significance behind his next, casually delivered words, than she could possibly realise. 'You must permit us to corrupt you a little.' Nodding at the hovering butler, he said, 'Three of the usual please, Hector.'

Going to a heavily stocked bar, the butler three-quarter filled sparkling crystal aperitif glasses and brought them to the fireplace area on a silver tray. 'We normally have dry sherry, from Jerez in Spain, for an appetiser,' Sophronia told Ellie, handing her a glass and taking one for herself, as she sat down next to her. 'It's most agreeable.'

Trying to appear very adult – which the closeted atmosphere of finishing school, although reputed to be an excellent preparation for adulthood seemed quite often to hold young ladies back from – Ellie raised the glass to her lips with a dimpled smile. She sipped tentatively, unsurprised to discover she liked the clean, cool taste.

Part of the Brexford master plan, of course, was to encourage Ellie, their intended victim, to over-indulge in alcohol; at dinner, after a main dish of partridge washed down with a heady red wine from Bordeaux, the strategy began to work. Ellie, in bubbling mood, was hanging on to every word from Jeremy and Sophronia, thoroughly intrigued by the pair of them. Their conversation had been witty and, in terms of her normally protected existence, somewhat provocative.

Ellie was staring with perhaps too much interest at Sophronia, the widening of her eyes and bouts of rapid blinking betraying an unaccustomed intake of liquor, when Sophronia said, 'I went to a finishing school, of course. They were very – strict.' She smiled disarmingly. 'How is the discipline at Chalmers, dear?'

'Horrible. We mayn't even wear make-up. I wouldn't have dared apply any for this evening, even if I had some.' Her eyes goggled over Sophronia's face, fixing for a moment on vermilion-painted lips. 'You look so, so lovely in yours.'

'But lovely without it, too – as you yourself, Ellie,' put in Jeremy.

'Ours was horrible too. Worse than awful, certainly. They even used to beat us.' She surveyed Ellie speculatively. 'Barbaric, when you think about it. Tell me, do girls get whipped at Chalmers?'

Ellie carefully crossed her Georgian silver knife and fork on her plate, keeping her eyes clearly focused by watching how the flickering candles in the chandelier above her head threw shadows of her fingers on the white linen at the edge of her plate. Slowly, she said, 'Whipped, no. But caned, yes. Often.'

'I was considered somewhat of a wicked girl, myself,' Sophronia told her. She caught Ellie's eyes as they rose from her finger-shadows to look at her curiously. 'I was at the wrong end of a flogging on several occasions. Nasty.' She emptied her glass, nodding to a servant who replenished it. Then, with a careless toss of her head and a deliberately demure smile at her husband she said, 'I used to take consolation afterwards in the arms of a girlfriend.' She paused, capturing Ellie's gaze. 'Do you understand what I mean?'

Confused, Ellie drained her glass, gaze dropping to Sophronia's peach lace-cosseted breasts, splendidly pushed forward by her bodice. She failed to reply to the question but her mind, fuzzy at the edges, raced. Whips and canes and girlfriends' arms – the conversation seemed to be taking an embarrassing but most interesting turn!

As Ellie's glass was topped up, Jeremy's eyes searched her keenly. The little dinner party, he decided, was progressing excellently. 'You must excuse my wife, Ellie,' he said. 'After a tipple or two she tends to come out with the most alarming confessions.'

'I, um, I really don't mind. I don't,' stammered Ellie, fearing that she was beginning to blush; but it was merely the effect of the wine which was bringing a slight flush to her cheeks – thereby adding to her attraction. She covered her awkwardness by hurriedly swallowing even more wine, an event which increased Jeremy's general satisfaction.

'I see nothing wrong in affectionate girlfriends kissing and cuddling one another – and so forth,' persisted Sophronia. She was sitting, defying custom, at the head of the long table, with her husband and Ellie facing each other on her left and right. Judging that the way was open for the beginnings of an advance, she dropped a hand to Ellie's blue satin-covered knee, squeezing it as she asked, 'What do you say, Ellie darling?'

The hand felt hot through her skirt. For the first time that evening Ellie, to whom a measure of her own sexual proclivities had but very recently been revealed sensed a certain wantonness in the atmosphere. Finding this confusingly agreeable, she was nevertheless incapable of any verbal response.

The exploring hand with its green-lacquered nails slid halfway up Ellie's thigh, gripping it hard; Sophronia's sexual intent was most obvious, Jeremy noted, with a gleam in his eye. 'Have you ever been caned yourself?' asked Sophronia.

Ellie's gaze darted from the hand on her leg, to Lady Brexford's revealing *décolleté*, and then to her face, where she dared herself to let it rest. Reminded of her thrashing and of the libidinous effect it had had on her, and intrigued by the hand which continued to burn through her skirt, Ellie realised without doubt that the evening's mood had turned cloyingly sexual; with her inhibitions thoroughly relaxed by the wine, she at last became a little bold. 'Caned? Yes I have been – just a few days ago,' she said, her eyes swivelling to those of Jeremy, losing themselves momentarily in their mysterious depths. 'It hurt tremendously, but I didn't mind it.'

'I see.' Sophronia's hand moved even higher, fingers clawing, digging into the softness of Ellie's upper thigh. 'And afterwards? Did you perhaps take – girlish comfort? With a friend?'

Her head was beginning to spin slightly. Ellie concentrated her gaze on the hand on her thigh, keeping it in focus but doing nothing to discourage it as she muttered, so quietly that the words were barely audible, 'Yes. Yes, I did. I did too.'

'Ahhh,' breathed Jeremy.

From then on events, that is to say advances from Lady and Lord Brexford, both of them deeply intent on seduction, passed in a kind of pleasantly hazy, arousing, erotic dream for Ellie, until she found herself, without knowing exactly how, in Sophronia's magnificent bedchamber being made comfortable on the crimson coverlet of her bed by Jeremy as Sophronia wound up her gramophone and put on a recording of a Scarlatti sonata.

The hauntingly erotic music filled the room. Gently raising Ellie's head, Jeremy slipped a cushion under it. Pleasantly cocooned in her alcoholic fuzz, eyes lazily exploring her new surroundings, Ellie felt almost as if she were floating. That Jeremy, perching on the edge of the bed beside her, should take one of her hands in both of his she found perfectly natural. Sophronia, who was gliding to the other side of the bed whilst gazing intently at her, she perceived as a vision of desirable loveliness.

Lady Brexford got on her knees at Ellie's side then lowered herself flat, cupping her chin in her hands and smiling. 'Cosy in here, is it not?' she murmured.

'It's a lovely room,' said Ellie.

'When was it exactly?'

'When was what?'

'Your caning.'

'Oh. Just four days ago.'

'Are you perhaps still sore?' asked Jeremy.

Ellie wriggled. She was indeed sore, a not altogether unpleasant reminder of the unexpectedly lustful experience. 'Just a little,' she said.

Sophronia shifted onto her side to face her, propping herself on one elbow. 'And you told us you have a girlfriend who comforted you afterwards,' she said huskily, eyelids fluttering. 'Tell me, did she do this?' She put a hand on Ellie's breast to gentle it.

Ellie momentarily tensed, then she shivered. Jeremy's hands tightened on hers. 'Yes,' she muttered.

'You really like that, don't you?' Sophronia planted a kiss on her cheek as she caressed her breasts.

'Mmmmm.'

'Skin to skin is much nicer.'

Nimble, eager fingers busied themselves. Seconds later the satin-covered buttons of Ellie's bodice were undone and it was pulled wide apart; her breasts, pale pink nipples hardening, were free. She experienced a moment's shame – for no man had ever seen her like that – but this quickly passed. An exquisite rush of pleasure surged through her as Sophronia stooped, flicked her tongue over a nipple and then sucked it into her mouth. Her hand fondled Ellie's other breast.

Jeremy elected to leave the bed and take a broader viewpoint. Sinking into an armchair nearby, he steepled his fingers, staring with engrossed, hooded eyes as his wife went skilfully to work, transferring her mouth from breast to breast, licking, sucking, teasing, biting. Both nipples became hard and pointy. Ellie, feeling deliciously, woozily wicked, rubbed her inner thighs together as her pussy throbbed with desire.

Replacing her mouth with a groping hand, Sophronia raised her head to kiss Ellie on the lips. It was one simple act which Georgina had neglected to perform and Ellie, who had only ever been kissed on the mouth once, by a clumsy, overheated boy and had been singularly unimpressed, a little disgusted even, found Sophronia's tender lips most sweet. As the kiss rapidly grew more passionate and Sophronia's tongue intruded into her mouth to find hers, it brought to her body libidinous sensations at least as arousing as the fondling of her breasts. Her nostrils flaring, Ellie began to respond in kind, her tongue prodding and probing as their saliva mingled.

It was the reaction Sophronia was looking for, the

signal to progress with her seduction. Her hand crept down over Ellie's belly, crawled over buttons yet done up, lingered over her crotch to press her skirt tight between her legs, travelled on to her ankles, slipped under the skirt hem and slid quickly back up over bare legs until it encountered heavy, brushed-cotton bloomers. She broke the kiss, leaving Ellie panting. 'And did your playmate also do this?' she whispered into Ellie's ear, finding her fleshy pussy lips which lay beneath the cotton with the tip of her middle finger.

Ellie drew in her breath sharply and let it out with a moan. Closing her eyes, she pushed her head back hard into the pillow, neck tautly stretched as she unconsciously willed the finger to explore further and find her wetness. Moments later, it had, wriggling its insistent way beneath the crotch of her knickers and slipping slowly inside her tight little hole. 'And this?' Sophronia breathed, stilling the finger.

'Oh God, yes.'

Ellie slightly raised her knees and parted her thighs, mewling, as Jeremy, cock stirring, asked softly, 'Is the wench good and wet?'

She had almost forgotten he was there, and the prurient words were a shocking reminder – they made her feel very dirty indeed. Ellie's hands flew to her breasts, rolling them sensuously together as Sophronia muttered, her finger on the move again, working its way over the little fold of hymen, 'Very wet, yes – and a virgin, as we had hoped.'

'But not for very much longer, I fear.' Lord Brexford muttered the words loudly enough for his own ears. He was not about to take the risk at this satisfactory stage of the proceedings of alarming Ellie with his ruttish intentions.

Convinced that there would be no resistance to

anything she might decide to do to the girl, Sophronia left her pussy alone to open the rest of the buttons of her dress. Throatily saying, 'It really won't do for you to return to your school with this all creased – we must have it off,' she swiftly relieved her of the garment, folding it carefully and lobbing it onto a chair.

'These, too,' she said, removing her shoes, dropping them on the floor.

With Ellie clad only in long, woolly green socks and her thick, white knickers, Sophronia hooked her fingers into the knicker waistband and dragged them in one pull to her knees, saying, 'And these.' Another pull and the bloomers were off, joining the shoes on the floor.

Sophronia changed both position and intent. She knelt between Ellie's legs, a hand on either knee parting them wide, as her eyes greedily explored the lewdly exposed pubis. She licked her lips and then murmured, 'I wonder if your girlfriend,' she paused, 'kissed you down there?'

Ellie's eyes sprang open. She ran them down her own nude body and up her raised thighs until they encountered Sophronia's. Feeling deliciously ribald and happily tipsy, she was past caring what happened to her, ready for anything that this randy pair might take it into their heads to subject her to – and for the third time in only four days, she discovered yet another bawdy aspect of her fast awakening sexuality. She found her tongue. 'What if she did?' she said brazenly.

'So. So.' Sophronia's eyes plundered the virgin parts. 'What wicked things girls do get up to.' She was filled with an irresistible craving to sample the delights of this sweet, not entirely innocent, pussy. 'If she did, then so shall I.'

Jeremy fiercely clutched his almost hard cock through his trousers, mumbling, 'That's it. That's it. Eat her Sophie. Tongue her cunt,' as his wife's predatory hands slipped from Ellie's knees down the insides of her thighs, and, reaching her pussy, spread its lips. Bending forward as if praying towards Mecca she began licking the little bud of Ellie's clitoris, her nose buried in a bunch of tight, pale brown pubic curls.

So aroused did Ellie become that her hands found the top of Sophronia's head to urge her on, and her socked feet lifted high to cross themselves over her raised behind. Sophronia interrupted her tongue's naughty business to lift her head against the pressure of Ellie's pushing and gaze steamily up at her through her milky tits. 'You know what "to come" means?' she asked.

'To, to have an orgasm?' gasped Ellie.

'Right. To get off. I am going to see just how speedily I can bring you off.' Her face dropped again. Her tongue licked over Ellie's clitoris and dived lower to find her vulva, to probe, to work its way within her pussy, going as deep as it was able. At the same time the balls of her index fingers pressed on either side of her hard, sensitive clitoris, jiggling it, masturbating her.

Bringing Ellie – who was in any case hovering on the brink – off took rather less than two minutes, as a tongue and fingers vastly more experienced than those of Georgina went determinedly to work. Then Ellie's feet slipped off Sophronia's backside to drop heavily on the scarlet bedspread; she arched her back, lifted her buttocks clean from the bed and, hands screwing into Sophronia's mussed hair, she cried out her climax to the canopy above as her pussy juices seeped over the tongue which filled her. Her mouth slackened, her eyes closed once more, her face sagged and she relaxed with a long and contented sigh.

Sophronia lifted her head with a wickedly triumphant smile at Jeremy, smudged vermilion lips glistening with saliva and pussy juice. Sinking back onto her heels she murmured. 'Well, the little girl is decidedly all for it. And now she is all yours, for a while at least, my lucky lover.'

Pulse racing, cock solid and begging to be released, Jeremy hauled himself to his feet and approached the bed as Sophronia made herself comfortable with her back propped on a pillow against the bedhead. Lady Brexford's pussy was, naturally, needful, but not so much that she craved immediate relief. Besides, she invariably found playing the voyeur most stimulating. Standing near Ellie's head, Jeremy laid a hand on her shoulder. 'Have you ever seen a naked man, Ellie?' he asked her softly. Her eyes opened wide on him.

Sudden modesty caused her to lower her legs and close them. She covered her pussy with a hand. 'No,' she mumbled.

'You'd like to though, I'd wager?'

Almost imperceptibly, she nodded – all the response he needed. He had already removed his jacket and waistcoat; now, eyes never leaving her, searching for a reaction, he stripped off his shirt, then his shoes and socks, then his trousers and, lastly, taking his time about freeing the buttons, his underpants.

The effect upon Ellie as a potent, full-blooded cock sprang into view was remarkable. At first she went so still she might have been paralysed. Then, fraction by fraction, her gaze fixed on Jeremy's genitals, her mouth opened until it formed a shocked 'O'. Finally, her intoxicated eyes slithered up the fine male body until they rested on his. The fingers which lay on her pussy twitched involuntarily.

'Well?' Lord Brexford asked, lustily expectant, cockhead pointing directly across Ellie at his wife's face. 'I trust that you don't find the sight of my family jewels disagreeable?'

'I . . .' Ellie slowly, fearfully, lowered her eyes until they once again lit on Jeremy's impressive, swollen member. She was suddenly aware of nothing else but genitalia; there was no room any more, no bed, no man even; her entire vision was filled with a monstrous cock and a heavy pair of balls surrounded by a great rug of black hair. In that moment it seemed that destiny spoke to her. And destiny was utterly lewd.

Jeremy shuffled forward until his kneecaps touched the bed, his wobbling prick half an arm's-length from Ellie's face. 'Should you so desire,' he told her, the words knifing into her belly, 'you may handle it. It is perfectly normal for a woman to behave in such a way with a man.'

Ellie, who had only, on rare occasion, read about such things, or discussed them with equally ignorant and innocent girlfriends, realised that she had been waiting since puberty for a moment such as this. She hesitated but briefly before, consumed with a libidinous curiosity, she stretched out a hand as her other one took a firmer grip on her pussy. Tentatively, with previously unexperienced thrills coursing through her, she put the ball of a finger on the side of Jeremy's shining glans – and then withdrew it sharply as if burnt when the cock swayed beneath her touch.

'Don't be afraid, Ellie,' said Jeremy, the words spilling hotly through his lips, 'it won't bite you. Take a good, firm hold of it.' Clutching her wrist, he pulled her hand onto him.

This time, she dared to wrap her fingers around it. He released her wrist to grab a breast almost fiercely. Surprised at the life which seemed to tremble within the turgid penis in her hand, at its faint throbbing, Ellie gasped. The mysterious object was muscularly hard, but she marvelled at the silky softness of its skin. 'I do believe, I do believe I . . . like it,' she mumbled hesitantly.

'And why not? It's supposed to be liked.' There was the merest shake in Jeremy's voice; he was becoming even more seriously aroused by the situation than his penis suggested. He massaged her breast a little more then hooked his hand behind her shoulder and pulled. 'Sit up, why don't you, and sample my testicles with your other hand?'

Confidence – and wantonness – increasing by the second, amazing feelings she had hardly even dreamed about tying her belly into a knot, Ellie did as she was asked, filling her wondering hands with a man's craving genitals. She found that, without consciously giving herself instructions, she was stroking the penis and squeezing the balls.

Sophronia watched avidly, hand buried beneath the folds of her skirt as she lazily fingered her very aroused pussy. 'The girl learns quickly,' she observed. 'Ellie, jerk your fist more – a man appreciates that. There's a splendidly rude word for it – do you know what it is?'

'To, to wank?' Ellie ventured as she moved her hand faster, becoming so excited that she began to tremble. 'I do know some things – I am eighteen.'

'My, my, you modern girls,' said Sophronia, raising an eyebrow. 'Actually, I was thinking of toss, but wank will do very nicely.' Her middle finger found its way inside herself, stabbing eagerly.

Jeremy groaned. His hips began to rock. He cradled both of Ellie's breasts, hissing, 'Do it, do it.'

'Perhaps you should ...?' began Sophronia, then stopped.

'Do what?' Ellie tore her eyes away from what she was doing to turn them on Lady Brexford, spotting her furtive masturbation as the rucked-up lace of her dress jumped.

Sophronia, who had been about to suggest that Ellie take her husband's cock into her mouth, decided that it was surely too early in the proceedings to introduce her to such matters; the girl might be truly shocked. Instead she softly said, 'Why don't you lie back on the bed and make yourself comfortable – and spread your legs good and wide?'

There was little confusion in Ellie's mind about what was next to befall her – nor was there any question of balking at it. A young woman's supreme moment was upon her. With an almost desperate craving to discover how the penis in her hand would feel in that begging place between her legs, she relinquished it, and his balls, to prostrate herself on the scarlet coverlet. Her head sunk into the down-filled pillow, her eyes blinked at the canopy above her.

The bed creaked noisily. Her vision became filled with Lord Brexford's head and shoulders as, knees between her shins, he lowered himself onto her. Taking his weight on his elbows, he brushed her breasts with his chest. His belly touched her pubis lightly. She was not, at that moment, aware of his cock, because it was indenting the bedspread between her open thighs. 'I shall be most gentle with you,' he promised, fighting to keep his voice steady. 'There will probably be a little pain, but this should soon pass.' He briefly kissed her lips. 'You are about to learn, Ellie, what life is truly about.'

'And there is no better teacher,' grunted Sophronia, a second finger joining the middle one in her pussy, the two pistoning.

Ellie took a very deep breath. Despite her willingness, she was becoming just a touch scared. As Jeremy lifted himself off her and reached for his cock, she glanced apprehensively down between their naked bodies. She saw him take hold of the weapon with which he was about to spear her, watched him position his glans so that it disappeared beneath her pubic mound. And then she felt it, her first ever experience of a cockhead easing into her pussy lips; so unlike the soft, warm wetness of the female tongue which had so recently left them that it seemed hard and dry. As it encountered her little fold of hymen it was unable, unlike the tip of a tongue or a finger, to slip comfortably by.

Very slowly, yet potently, with the same great care he was accustomed to exercising at the start of sodomy, Jeremy pushed, his glans stretching the tiny membrane fraction by fraction towards breaking point.

Ellie yelped. She closed her eyes. There was some pain – but it was bearable, if not in itself as arousing as had been that of the caning. It increased to the point where it caused her to cry out, then it suddenly went into retreat. At last she felt a cock, thick, warm, filling her pussy more than she had known it could be filled, breaching her tight, moist, virgin canal. Up and up in her it went until she felt sure it was going to poke its way right into her womb; then it stilled.

She opened her eyes. Jeremy was poised rigidly over her on straight arms, a hand indenting the coverlet on either side of her shoulders. Their pubic bushes, she saw, were intermingled – then she realised that that big cock was buried inside her in its entirety.

'All right?' he grunted. 'All right, Ellie?'

'Oh God,' she moaned, hardly aware of her words. 'Oh shit, oh God. Don't ever stop. Don't ever stop.' Dark tales of the blood and pain of this moment were frequently whispered about the school. A little pain there had been and it lingered, blood there might be, but there was no evidence of it pouring out of her. Her overwhelming emotions were a gloriously heady triumph at having finally met her destiny and a sexual fire, hotter than that which had burned her thrashed behind, raging inside her belly.

Jeremy withdrew until only his cockhead was within her. They both peered down between their bodies to see that there was a small smear of blood on his cock. 'Good,' he mumbled, further, feverishly aroused by this revelation. 'Good, good.' Then he slipped his length slowly all the way into her again. He paused, noting in satisfaction the way she was panting and drooling, and that her hands were screwing up the pillow on either side of her head; then his buttocks jerked and he began to fuck her in earnest.

Feeling restricted by her clothes, craving nakedness as she watched the relentless rise and fall of her husband's bare behind, Sophronia speedily slipped out of her garments, strewing them carelessly over the floor. Clambering off the bed, overcome with salaciousness, she took a small, silken, padded chair from her dressing table, positioned it near the foot of the bed below the rutting couple and sank down onto it. She lifted her feet to rest them on either side of the soles of those of her husband, knees apart. In that way she had a clear, provocative view between her thighs of vigorously bouncing balls and the appearing and disappearing underside of Jeremy's cock as he pounded Ellie seriously. As she watched she masturbated steadily, two middle fingers back to back inside her pussy and both thumbs on her clitoris. It was the first time she had actually witnessed her husband in the act of deflowering a girl; Sophronia was finding the singular event most incredibly bawdy.

Ellie reached orgasm fractionally before Jeremy, and voiced it with a noisy, protracted squeak. Moments later, as her thighs convulsed and trembled on the outside of his, and her hands went limp on the pillow, she became aware that he had withdrawn and that a warm wetness was hitting her inner thighs, and then her taut belly. She looked down to see that Jeremy's cock, grasped firmly in his hand, was erupting all over her nether regions, an activity she observed in horny fascination. Then it was spent, and he rolled away from her onto his back with a long and heavy sigh.

Sophronia's frigging had become so in tune with the rhythm of the screw that she had climaxed at exactly the same time as Ellie. As Ellie's toes uncurled and she turned a blissful, wanton smile towards the canopy, Sophronia left her chair to crawl up beside her on the bed. She flattened her hand on Ellie's belly over a sticky puddle of her husband's semen and began, with a circular motion, to work it into her skin. Kissing her cheek she told her, with a voice so husky it might have been that of a boy in the act of breaking, 'Jeremy is such a considerate man. He didn't want to give you a baby, you see, so he ejaculated outside your fanny.'

'God. I never even thought about that,' Ellie muttered.

'No, but he did.'

Lord Brexford – who perhaps had not been particularly considerate in his timely withdrawal as much as coarse in his desire at the moment of orgasm to besmirch Ellie's flesh with his seed – sat up. His eyes raked over the two naked females. Then he glanced from Ellie's thighs, where a little watery blood mingled with his semen, to his wilted cock with its red evidence of spoiled virginity. He said, casually, recovered from orgasm remarkably speedily, 'Very little bleeding then. So often the case.' A self-satisfied smile flitted across his face. 'Well, this would seem to call for a celebration.' Reaching to the back of the bed he tugged at a tasselled bell rope. Then he twisted around, put his lips close to the mouthpiece of a voice tube on the wall and called for champagne and glasses to be left outside the bedroom door.

Sophronia draped an arm over Ellie's torso and cushioned her face on her breast, staring up at her. 'I don't have to ask you if you enjoyed that,' she said, her voice just as sexily husky. 'Clearly you did.' She kissed the breast. 'Are you very sore?'

So overwhelmed with what had happened to her and so replete after her two orgasms was Ellie that she had not yet begun to consider the state of her vagina. Now she did. She found that there was a certain amount of discomfort there, but this was more than compensated for by her marvellously satiated libido. 'I am a bit sore, yes, Sophronia,' she replied. 'But I do believe that I'm very happy about it.'

'Are you now. I admire your self-confidence.' Sophronia glanced across Ellie's bosom to her husband. 'The girl has become very sure of herself, has she not, Jeremy?'

'Not blushing for shame, as might have been the case, thank God.' Still most pleased with the success of his manly enterprise, he smirked as he fiddled with

103

Ellie's nipple. 'You are going to make a lot of men very happy, do you know that?'

Ellie briefly considered that prospect and pulled a wry face. 'And I had thought there would be just one special man.'

'No doubt there will be, in time. But you must sow your wild oats properly first. I know your type, Ellie – a randy young thing, and nothing whatsoever wrong in that.' There was a loud rap on the door. Jeremy swung his legs to the floor. 'That'll be the bubbly.'

Sitting cross-legged on the huge four-poster bed in glimmering fire and candle light and wearing only her green woollen socks, sharing champagne with this naked lord and his equally naked lady having just parted with her virginity, Ellie felt that she had been, and was being, extraordinarily wicked. She therefore searched her soul for remorse – but she found none. Rather, she seemed to have met destiny head on and to have come completely to terms with it. This carnal evening was the culmination of her week of self-discovery; in a slightly euphoric, alcoholic fuddle she might have been, but her head was clear enough for her to know that she was feeling shamelessly raunchy and that she was filled with ribald anticipation of what her lusty hosts would get up to with her next.

Suddenly Jeremy tipped some champagne onto the insides of her thighs, making her giggle. Then taking a handkerchief from the bedside table he first dabbed away her bloodstains, then refolded it, poured a little more champagne on it and cleaned his penis. 'Congratulations,' he said, touching glasses with her. 'Here's to lost innocence.'

Sophronia also chinked her glass with Ellie's. 'I'll drink to that,' she laughed. 'And good riddance, say I.'

'Now that you are no longer a virgin it will be necessary for you to begin to learn something about the art of sex.' Jeremy's eyes were wandering restlessly over Ellie's body. 'Sophronia and I volunteer to be your mentors.'

Ellie's pulse raced. She was enormously aware of her pussy, which, despite its slightly disagreeable soreness, seemed to be pleading for another fuck. She mumbled, 'I must not return to Chalmers too late.'

'Indeed. But there will be other evenings – many of them, I hope. As for what remains of this one I think, well, an object lesson, perhaps?'

As he got out of his squatting position, Jeremy drained his glass and put it on the table. Then he walked on his knees to Sophronia's feet which were crossed Indian fashion in front of her, with his cock, spurred on by further risqué thoughts again on the rise. 'Let us continue with Ellie's education,' he said, slipping his hand under Sophronia's hair at the nape of her neck, pulling her face forward and down.

Sophronia wetted her lips. 'So very soon after humping her?' she murmured. 'My my, aren't we turned on tonight?'

'Aren't we just. But don't think I am not mindful of your own unsatisfied needs.' He glanced at Ellie with a slack smile. 'You are about to witness one of the most exciting ways that a woman may stimulate a man.' He shoved his cock at Sophronia's pouting lips which she opened, drawing the glans into her mouth with her tongue.

Blinking furiously at the scene, Ellie gulped down her champagne. She took the liberty of reaching for the bottle and replenished her glass shakily, watching in disbelief as, with evident relish, Sophronia sucked on Jeremy's rapidly hardening prick. She had read references to such an act in *Justine* but had assumed it to be pure, depraved fantasy, refusing to believe that a woman could be so lewd – and now the thing was happening in front of her startled eyes. What was more, witnessing this, seeing Lord Brexford's buttocks rock as his penis moved within his wife's mouth failed to have any negative effect on her: on the contrary, it brought an even greater longing to her pussy, making her forget its soreness altogether. Her hand dropped between her legs. She began to caress herself.

By the time that, minutes later, Lord and Lady Brexford were head to tail next to her and eating one another as if their lives depended on it, Ellie, face drooping in utter wantonness, eyes riveted on the fervent sixty-nine, was masturbating with as much enthusiasm as she had mustered whilst reading the pages of that forbidden book.

After a while, the two tired of that particular activity. Jeremy rolled onto his back and Sophronia sank down onto his hard-on, facing him, bouncing on it. From then on, whilst carrying on as if Ellie were not present, they were especially turned on by the fact that she was, passionately copulating in varied positions, presenting the girl with a sort of mini, live version of the *Kama Sutra*. They made it last for more than half an hour during which Ellie, wallowing in a most agreeable mire of dissoluteness, frigged herself to orgasm three times and then gasped her way through the fourth as her wanton hosts climaxed together, doggie-fashion. Jeremy collapsed across Sophronia's back as she flattened out onto her belly.

Fifteen minutes later, Sophronia had crawled between her sheets, Jeremy was in a dressing-gown and Ellie was fumbling to do up her satin buttons. Offering Ellie pleasantries as if nothing out of the way had occurred, Jeremy rang for his chauffeur to take her home. Completely overcome by all that had happened to her, Ellie could find nothing at all to say.

As they awaited the chauffeur, Jeremy said, 'We must get together again very soon. But first you must give your fanny a few days to recover. In any case, I have to go up to London.' His jaundiced eye burnt through her dress. 'You would like to see us again?'

Contradictorily and annoyingly, Ellie found that she was blushing faintly. 'Yes. Yes, I would,' she managed.

Sophronia raised her head a fraction from her pillow. 'Did you not remark, Ellie, during dinner, that you didn't mind when you were caned?' she asked sleepily, as the chauffeur rapped on the door.

Chapter Eight

One purpose of Lord Brexford's staying over for a few days in London was to take care of several matters pertaining to a number of valuable family properties in the city. But a more interesting aspect of his sojourn was the opportunity it provided him for plentiful indulgence of his capacious sexual appetite.

In a small, attractive town house, an insignificant part of his vast estate, at Hyde Park Square – but a stone's throw from the Bayswater Road and the great park itself – he had recently installed a most pliant, beautiful, sensual and adventurous mistress. Her name was Charlotte – it amused him to call her Charlie – and the fact that she was of common stock merely added to his pleasure in, and indulgence of her. Anticipating the theme of *Pygmalion* by five or so years – perhaps George Bernard Shaw whom he counted amongst his intimate circle of friends eventually took the idea from him – Jeremy was attempting, in Professor Higgins fashion, to perform the near miracle of turning a commoner into a gentlewoman.

Charlotte was never forewarned of when her lover and benefactor was going to pay her a visit, a deliberate stratagem on Jeremy's part to keep other men out of – and off – his property. With her, he strove for the sort of sexual domination he had achieved with Sophronia, that was to allow her dalliance with hungry males only at his whim and in his presence. For her part, Charlotte was terrified to jeopardise her new found position of privilege, and in the three months since the fortuitous arrangement, she had been assiduous in refusing all masculine advances. Besides which, she was deeply infatuated with her noble peer of the realm and would do anything to please him.

When her door bell jangled three times late on the afternoon of her twice weekly piano lesson, she knew by its sound that it could only be him. She dismissed the teacher immediately; on his way out, the man hurried by Lord Brexford as he was let in by the maid. Not bothering to remove anything besides his hat in the hall, Jeremy brought with him, on his heavy top-coat, a touch of autumn chill into the chintzy drawing room; a dead leaf from a chestnut tree adorned his dark grey cashmere shoulder.

He quickly stripped off his gloves, his experienced eye appreciating this very tall and slender, auburn-haired hidden treasure as she snaked towards him, her large, eminently kissable lips smiling a warm, genuine welcome.

'But who was that old man who was in such a hurry to leave?' Jeremy asked her.

She brushed the leaf off his shoulder and unfastened the top button of his coat, mouth upturned towards his expectantly. 'Why, my piano teacher,' she told him, 'you wanted me to have lessons, remember?'

'Ah, yes.' Her elocution he noted, gratified, seemed to have improved markedly in the more than two weeks since he had last visited her. But he was in for a small disappointment in that direction. 'Just so long as he was not some secret lover or other.'

'Don't be bloody daft!' she exclaimed.

With an exasperated laugh he drew her close to him. He kissed her long and tenderly on the mouth. Then, holding her at arm's length as she finished the job of unbuttoning his coat he said, 'A lady would say, "Don't be so damned silly," my dear Charlie.'

She pulled a rueful face. 'Maybe she would. But then a lady would hardly be called Charlie.'

'She might. In any case, you are. You're my delightful Charlie.'

He turned his back on her so that she could remove his coat, then watched her lustily as she took it and his gloves to the door and summoned her maid to get rid of them; she was possessed, he considered, of the sensuousness of a gazelle. Her haunches, swelling sexily to fill perfectly the green and yellow gingham of her dress, maddened him with their sway as she walked. Her thick and wavy hair glinted as it rippled down to the small of her elegant back.

She closed the door firmly on her maid – a clear indication that she was not to be disturbed – and returned to him. Taking her once again in his arms he kissed her with passion, his tongue probing her mouth to mingle with hers, his hips grinding fiercely against her. In her medium-heeled, black patent leather boots, just visible beneath the hem of her skirt, Charlotte was as tall as he. As their pubises responded to the sensual clash, she could feel him hardening beneath the heavy tweed of his trousers.

'Needful?' she murmured, into his mouth.

He broke the kiss to push her away from him, hands cupping and fondling her breasts as his penetrating gaze swept up and down her body. 'Of course. As always with you. Who would not be?'

She wrinkled her delightful nose at him teasingly, and her large eyes, their soulful brown a similar col-

our to his own, searched his face. 'I'm sure I dunno
– oops – I don't know.'

'It seems you are not yet ready to be taken into
polite society.'

'You may take me anywhere which pleases you.'
This time she was most deliberate with her diction,
almost, but not quite, sounding the perfect lady. Her
enunciation of the word 'take' strayed fractionally in
the undesirable direction of 'tike', but she made a
perfect job of pronouncing the 'h' in 'anywhere'.

He turned her breasts as if he were twiddling large
doorknobs. 'And take you anyhow which pleases me.'

She gasped. He had a way with words and simple
sexual actions, with his powerful charisma, of arousing her as no man had ever managed prior to him.
'Shall I undress for you?' she whispered.

His Adam's apple wobbled with the sudden constriction of his throat. 'Everything. I want to see you,
to have you, without a stitch on.'

His craving was catered for without any attempt at
protracted performance. In less than a minute Charlotte stood before him in her breathtaking nakedness,
her dress, camisole top, underskirt and white, silken
camiknickers in a heap at her feet, topped off carelessly by her boots.

Jeremy produced a heavy, desire-choked sigh. His
eyes raked her body from head to toe before latching
hungrily onto the thick, coppery bush of her pussy,
his cock almost in pain as, grown solid, it strained
against the tight constriction of thick, woollen underpants and tweed trousers. Only two paces divided her
from him. Taking one, he reached down to hook the
tips of his fingers between her legs and eased the
middle one up into her fleshily soft pussy lips and the
anticipated dampness there. She made a little mewl-

111

ing noise, a pampered cat, flawless thighs trembling on his hand. But she held her voice deliberately steady, eyes raunchily challenging his as she asked, accustomed to the immediacy of his libidinous requirements whenever he visited, 'How then would you like to possess me, my lord?'

His finger probed deeper, to the second knuckle, jerking within her as if beckoning, making her wetter by the second. With his other hand he fumbled at his fly buttons, almost tearing them apart in his sudden eagerness. His eyes speedily roved the room and narrowed, glinting with lust as they came to rest. 'The piano,' he grunted, 'bend over it. Now.'

Charlotte took the few steps to her Steinway baby grand. She scooped a cushion from its bow-legged, ornamental stool and, throwing a fire-filled glance over her shoulder at Jeremy, flattened her breasts over the cushion on the piano top. With her hips resting in its elegant, concave curve, she spread her legs just enough to afford her lover a perfect rear view of her pussy. Reaching down between her legs, her cheek squashed against gleaming, varnished wood, she did something that she knew would drive him wild in that torrid moment, an action which had much the same effect on herself; with two fingers she opened her pussy lips wide.

Perfectly still in that most wanton and provocative of poses, Charlotte waited expectantly. Jeremy, rampant, did not even bother to unfasten his belt. He feverishly hauled his swollen cock and heavy balls free of their restricting garments. Gripping the cock around its thick root he closed in on Charlotte's soft, smooth and coltish thigh backs, tight, white buttocks and lewdly proferred hole. For the briefest of moments he rubbed his glans up and down the crack of her behind, teasing her puckered little anus with it. Then he fitted it between her two widely parted, pussy-framing knuckles and plunged.

He went in with such lust-driven force, all the way up her until his balls crammed themselves against her thighs, that for a moment he hurt her delicate flesh; she was jammed into the edge of the Steinway, and she cried out.

'Shut up, Charlie,' he hissed, his ingrained streak of sadism which she had very quickly learned about – and taught herself to enjoy – taking over, 'just shut your pretty mouth while . . .' He drew all the way out, smearing a trace of vaginal juice up her buttock crack, positioned himself and slammed into her again, '. . . I ram it into you just as hard as I like.'

Her hands took a firm grip of the opposite edge of the piano, knuckles whitening as she steeled herself for the coming assault. With his cock buried in her and momentarily still, she jabbed the tips of her fingers surrounding his heavy penis-root hard into his balls, further inflaming him as she muttered, 'Do me any way you like – but just do me, filthy bastard,' knowing that was the sort of response that he loved.

He fucked her with such vigour that the baby grand, which stood on a Chinese rug atop a polished oak floor, began to creep across the room. By the time he came inside her, only minutes later, with a bellow so loud it reached the scandalised ears of the maid in the kitchen, the piano had moved almost a yard. As her pussy was filled with the warm, sticky, glorious flood and the echo of Jeremy's yell faded away, Charlotte, overcome with a massive orgasm of her own, also shouted; the maid, who had never heard such things until being employed in this house, went very still, fingers digging hard into her bicep.

Jeremy sagged, taking his weight on his hands on the Steinway, panting, perspiration beading his brow, prick, dribbling still, nestled full in Charlotte's relaxing pussy. Her breath had steamed the varnish in front of her cheek somewhat and she had also dribbled on it, but she could nevertheless make out the reflection of her languid eye. The thought drifted idly through her head that nobody had fucked her previously in the ways Lord Brexford contrived; it had almost always been on her back in, or on, a bed – not that, at just twenty, she was a young lady of great experience. Even now he was milking the last drops of pleasure for them both by staying in her, his thighs rubbing against hers, his hips knocking into her buttocks and balls gently bumping as his cock slowly wilted. It had admittedly been a most rapid screw, but nevertheless it had been wonderful.

At last Jeremy withdrew his cock to smear the last drops of semen over Charlotte's buttocks, then he slipped it away inside his trousers with a sigh of luxurious content. As she, equally replete and happy, straightened up to turn and face him, he said with an enigmatic smile, 'But don't get dressed yet. Let me hear what *else* you have learnt on the piano, naked lady. Then we may take a perfumed bath together and afterwards have a meal in that nice little restaurant in Knightsbridge. After that,' he pursed his lips as she perched on the piano stool to perform for him what little she knew – which consisted largely of simple scales, 'after that I have the most scandalous of evenings planned.'

Having taken her for an early dinner without revealing further what those plans might be, Jeremy surprised Charlotte by having them driven in a hansom, not, as she was half expecting, to some ill-famed house or other, but back to Hyde Park Square. But they were not destined to remain at the town house for long; he had the cab wait. Inside, he marched her directly into her bedroom where he opened her wardrobe doors and began rummaging through her clothes.

'Yes,' he told her, finding what he wanted, 'this I believe will do very nicely indeed.' He tossed her the top half of a fine, black velvet two-piece, a long-sleeved bodice with a fancy ruffle around the neck and down the front, and high, padded shoulders.

'This will be the third time I've changed today,' she said, uncomplaining, as she caught it, dropped it on a chair and removed her ankle-length, ermine coat. 'But as it happens, you've picked one of my favourite outfits. Please give me the skirt.'

'No. Not the skirt.' He mouthed a wicked grin.

'But it doesn't go with the one I'm wearing.'

'No it doesn't. So take it off.'

She hesitated only fractionally. 'Wh'ever you want.'

'Whatever,' he corrected her, mildly.

She quickly stripped to a waspish, button-up corset, pink bloomers and heavy white stockings held up with scarlet garters. She started to slip an arm into the sleeve of the velvet bodice. He stopped her.

'Take the corset off first.'

'But I'll be cold.'

'You'll be warmed up.'

When she had the top on, she did a pirouette for him. It nipped in attractively at her slender waist only to flare over her hips. 'Now what?' she asked.

Again he searched in her wardrobe to produce a pair of knee-length, black leather boots with spiky

115

high heels and silver buttons down their sides. He took them to her, thrusting them into her hands. 'These,' he said. His eye roamed up and down her legs. 'But without the stockings.'

'You want me to bloody freeze.'

He raised an amused eyebrow. 'In ermine? Besides, I'm taking us somewhere hellishly torrid.'

The fire in the bedroom grate had burned very low. Charlotte shivered as she sat on the edge of the bed, took off her shoes, rolled off her stockings and pulled on the boots. Jeremy watched with the keenest of interest as she buttoned up the extraordinarily sexy boots. When they were in place, he cast an eye over her hair which she had piled up gracefully for dinner. He told her he wanted it down, which she did without protest in front of her dressing-table mirror. When she had finished brushing it he had her stand facing him.

'I don't believe you need knickers, Charlie,' he said.

'We are going out, aren't we?'

'So we are. Just the same.' He dropped on one knee in front of her to ease her bloomers down, over the boots and off. The bottom of her bodice just reached the top of her coppery thatch of pubic hair, nicely emphasising the purest of white flesh surrounding her pussy. Briefly, bloomers dangling from his hand, he clutched her around her buttocks and licked between her legs, making her shiver from more than the chill, the tips of his fingers digging into the crack of her behind. He looked up at her as he teased her bottom hole. 'We are going to have quite an evening, you and I,' he muttered.

There seemed to be something deliciously depraved about sitting in the back of a horse-drawn hansom cab as it rattled through the streets of London, cosseted in ermine whilst naked beneath it – apart from

116

her boots – below the waist; the very circumstances, combined with the fact of having no idea where they were bound except that it was sure to be some den of depravity of other, contrived to make Charlotte – a most libidinous young lady under any circumstances – exceptionally horny.

It was slightly foggy. After fifteen minutes or so of being driven at a smart trotting pace over cobbled streets, Charlotte had no idea of where they were. In fact they were north of Regent's Park, heading up the Finchley Road towards Hampstead. After the same length of time again, during which Jeremy laid not a finger on Charlotte's person – though she wished that he would – they stopped in front of a gloomy-looking terraced house in a street just off Hampstead Heath.

They were admitted to the house by a man dressed entirely in black except for a white shirt. He was half a head taller than Jeremy, very lean and straight-backed, and at first Charlotte took him to be a servant until he introduced himself to her as Count Alexis Petrovski. With few words he showed them in to an overfurnished, dowdy room, and had them sit in brown leather armchairs as he promptly left them on their own.

'Alexis is exiled aristocracy from some Eastern European country or other. I've never quite made out where,' Jeremy explained.

'I find him sort of spooky,' commented Charlotte. 'The way he walks with a kind of a glide. And he has a sorcerer's face.'

Jeremy smiled flatly. 'Observant of you. He is a sort of a sorcerer. He likes to play the high priest in black magic ceremonies, that sort of thing. My wife, as I believe I've told you, has been dabbling in that nonsense of late. She's had instruction from both

Alexis and Aleister Crowley. She seems to find it enormously amusing.'

'Is that what we came here for, then – witchcraft?' asked Charlotte, more curious than concerned.

His eyes wandered restlessly over her. 'Not on this occasion, no. We are here for – let us call it sexcraft.'

The Count returned, a black Persian cat padding by his side. The way he moved, he appeared to be as light as the cat. Charlotte noticed with a slight start that around the animal's neck there hung an ornamental silver cross, and that it was upside down. Petrovski went to a black iron fireplace where he stoked a rather listless fire into life and added more coals as the cat promptly curled itself in front of it and went to sleep. Watching him, Charlotte found it impossible to judge his age; he might have been anywhere between thirty-five and fifty-five. He seemed to sense her inspection because as he straightened up, his eye, cutting icily, darted directly to her face. He spoke in a husky voice, the accent heavy, to ask her why she did not remove her cloak.

His frank stare unnerved her, though she decided that his facial features, despite their somewhat satanical lines, were not unattractive. Acutely aware of her nakedness beneath the cloak, she was stumped for an answer. Her eyes swivelled frowningly to Jeremy. As she might have expected, he did not mince his words. 'Charlie is naked from her waist to the top of her boots,' he said. 'My idea, naturally.'

'Of course, your idea. You are thinking I do not know your ingenious mind by now?' Count Petrovski's coal-black eyes stabbed into Charlotte's, their coldness relieved by a faint trace of amusement. 'You are perhaps finding your state of undress – provocative?'

Charlotte, not about to admit to a perfect stranger that she indeed found the situation sexually titillating, rose admirably to the challenge. 'I don't provoke easily, Count. But I like to do whatever Jeremy finds pleasing.'

'Most admirable. Perhaps it would then please Jeremy if you now . . .' his gaze brushed speculatively over the ermine, '. . . remove the cloak?'

Lord Brexford was busy lighting a cigar. He dropped the match in an ashtray and puffed twice before saying, 'Very shortly, Alexis. Perhaps you wouldn't mind containing your natural curiosity until the arrival of your young friend?'

'As you wish.' The doorbell rang. 'But here is Arnold now.'

The Count slipped through the door into the passage. Standing up, Jeremy took Charlotte's hand and pulled her to her feet; he undid the neck of her cloak and swiftly took it off her. Taking her to the fireplace, he had her lean by the side of it, her hands behind her back and her legs spread seductively. 'Try and look casual,' he told her, 'as if there was nothing at all untoward about your mode of attire.'

It had happened so quickly that Charlotte had no time for embarrassment. She tried to think nothing whilst realising that in her vulgar exposure, she must present the picture of a blatant streetwalker exhibiting her wares. She appeared studiedly relaxed, but as she heard the sound of footsteps echoing in the hall, her insides began to seethe with nerves; Jeremy had several times inveigled her into odd and steamy scenes, but up until now he had never contrived to have her act in such an utterly lewd, brazen fashion.

The two men both noticed her at once as they came through the door and paused on the threshold, eyes popping. There was a long moment of silence, during which the cat woke up, yawned, stretched, and went back to sleep. Charlotte could sense the men's eyes scorching over her naked pussy, but could not bring herself to look at them; her gaze remained fixed on a burn mark on the dull grey rug beneath her feet. Jeremy broke the silence with words which knifed her. 'Come now, Charlie,' he said, 'what do you find so interesting about the floor? Say hello to Arnold.'

Her head, as she lifted it, felt heavy as lead. Her eyes fell uncertainly on the new arrival and when she saw he was no older than her, for some reason she felt very ashamed. She tried to smile a greeting and failed, managing only a curt nod.

'Hello, Charlie,' said Arnold a prurient grin on his almost baby-face, the palest of blue eyes jumping from hers to her crotch and back again.

'The young lady is not easily provoked,' observed the Count, cynically. 'Are you, my dear?'

The words had the effect of pulling Charlotte marginally together. She thrust her chin defiantly at him. 'No, I'm not.'

'Then why do you not relax?' He closed the door without taking his eyes from her. 'You are here, most clearly, to indulge in sex; why else come dressed as you are?' He drifted over to her with his curious walk, frankly gloating at her bare loins. 'Timidity ill becomes a wench who has a fanny made to be admired by all men.' He crouched before her, face inches from her crotch. 'I do not believe that I have seen such a red-haired fanny in many years.' His breath tickled the tops of her thighs. 'A most sensuous little kitten of a fanny.' Without looking at Lord Brexford, he asked, 'Do you mind, Jeremy?'

Charlotte watched her lover, belly churning. The situation was most unnerving. She could easily have rushed from the room, but so besotted was she with Jeremy that she stood her ground as he said, 'Go ahead, my dear Count. Sample Charlotte's wares as you will. She is as much my contribution to this evening's sport as Arnold is yours.'

'Well, I shall make just the briefest acquaintance for the moment.'

Alexis Petrovski's hands, long, bony, ascetic, with shiny pink, finely manicured nails, chilled Charlotte's inner thighs as he further parted them. Charlotte watched the top of his thinly black-haired head in confusion as he moved his face into her. She expected his tongue to come out, but he touched her not with that but with the tip of his thin, aristocratic nose. He rubbed it over her clitoris, buried it below between her pussy lips, then brought it up through her bush with a rapid shake of his head like a dog shaking its wet coat. Her tummy grew tense as he pulled up her bodice to expose her navel, and the nose travelled up the narrow line of red hair from her pussy to dip into it and sniff deeply before parting company with her flesh. Two fingers then traced their way back down the route taken by his nose until they arrived at her pussy lips, and wormed their tips in.

Charlotte's demeanour was changing rapidly. The sheer lubricity of having this peculiar man, until no more than ten minutes ago unknown to her, on his knees at her bared cunt, finally disposed of her nervousness – and her indifference.

As the fingers probed, she felt herself growing damp. He stood, squeezing her pussy, fingertips remaining inside, eyes boring down into hers as he muttered, 'We may not be exactly kings, you and I, Jeremy, but you bring me a cunt fit for royalty.' Then, leaving her faintly weak, he unhanded her and moved away.

121

'Why don't you sit down now, Charlie?' she heard Jeremy say. 'You seem to have got the party off to a most satisfactory beginning.' He joined the broad-shouldered, narrow-hipped Arnold on a worn, brown leather sofa. Charlotte, aroused, and no longer experiencing any shame, walked boldly to an armchair near the fire.

As she sank into the chair and crossed her legs so that only the merest tuft of pussy hair was on display, a tiny red vee, Charlotte cast her eyes over Arnold, seeing him clearly for the first time. He was so pretty, she saw, that he looked almost androgynous. Jeremy's arm was over his shoulders and as she noticed the way in which he was looking at the young man, she suddenly remembered her lover's ribald tales of boyish homosexuality at Eton. Perhaps, then, Arnold was indeed a homosexual and a side of Jeremy carried over from school days was about to be revealed? She smiled to herself, prepared, now, for any sort of vice on what she had been promised was to be a most scandalous evening.

'I must light the gas fires to warm the attic,' said Count Petrovski. 'It will be cold up there. Meanwhile Arnold might play for us.' Before leaving the room he produced a violin case from a corner, opened it and took the violin and bow to the young man.

'The attic?' echoed Charlotte as the door closed.

'The most interesting room in what is otherwise a rather disgustingly gloomy house, as you will shortly see,' Jeremy told her. He drew on his cigar and flicked it, half-consumed, into the fire as he watched Arnold who, perched on the arm of the sofa, was plinking the strings as he tuned the instrument.

A few minutes later, when the Count returned to open the drawer of a bureau and take from it a slender clay pipe, Arnold was playing – and doing so beautifully. 'Paganini, "Caprice Number Nine", observed Petrovski. 'Arnold is as good a musician as he is a ballet dancer. I envy him his talent so much. Now ...' he opened the top of a porcelain jar on the bureau, 'we will all enjoy a little smoke. Lovely music and opium together will temper our mood.'

The Count filled the pipe and lit its contents, taking a long, deep drag, inhaling, holding the smoke down with eyes closed then slowly exhaling as he took the pipe to Jeremy. They each indulged in the favourite vice of Conan Doyle's Baker Street detective; Charlotte, inexperienced in such matters, coughed. As Arnold passed the pipe on to begin another round, Petrovski stopped him from continuing with his piece. 'I think,' he said, 'that it is perhaps unfair when only one of my two young guests is displaying her genitals. Perhaps we might all enjoy the music the more with the violinist nude?'

Arnold shrugged carelessly. 'If you wish.' He laid down the violin and bow, got to his feet and quickly stripped to the buff, draping his clothes over an empty chair as he did so. Naked, he exhibited a typically beautiful ballet dancer's body in which every muscle was powerfully defined and upon which not only Charlotte's eyes lingered with longing. Between his knotted, bulging thighs nestled a plump pair of testicles and a short, fat, uncircumcised penis. His pubic hair was shaved. Curious about this, and noticing the lascivious looks on the other men's faces as they studied the Greek god-like body, Charlotte reasoned that the evening was perhaps going to offer her acts beyond her previous knowledge. She was not left to wonder for long about Arnold's lack of pubic hair because Petrovski said, having luxuriously inhaled more opium, 'Excellent. You did as I requested with your razor.'

Arnold glanced down at himself. 'I rather like the feeling,' he said. Tucking the violin beneath his chin, he parked his bare behind on the sofa arm and resumed his playing. He was facing Charlotte with legs spread, therefore offering her a perfect view of his cock and balls. Noticing the way he looked at her she realised that the blatant genital display was deliberate and that, although Arnold might be queer he was probably not exclusively so. Beginning to feel heady from the effects of the drug, she mischievously uncrossed her legs to offer him a reciprocal view of her pussy.

Twenty minutes and one more pipeload of opium later, they were all feeling splendidly mellow. Arnold was standing by then, enthusiastically performing a piece from Tchaikovsky, swaying his body to the rhythms, muscles rippling, cock wobbling, whilst the others silently appreciated both music and flesh, their eyes somewhat glazed. Now that she was not alone in it, Charlotte was most happy with her nakedness. She was aroused by the ribaldry which lay heavy in the air; almost without her being aware of it, the fingers of her right hand had curled into her pussy and were gentling it as her woozy mind drifted into speculation about what might shortly occur up in the mysterious attic.

The moment arrived. Arnold came to the end of a tune; Petrovski nodded significantly at him and he took the violin to its case and shut it away. 'It will be comfortably warm upstairs now,' said the Count, 'I suggest we proceed with what is the evening's main objective.' Getting to his feet, he took hold of Charlotte's hand and pulled her up; her other hand fell away from her pussy and flopped onto her thigh. 'We have all observed you playing with your glorious fanny,' he murmured. 'This will no longer be necessary.'

'Or even possible,' added Jeremy.

'Lead the way, Arnold,' said the Count. He dropped Charlotte's hand to recharge his pipe. 'Follow him up, Charlie.'

Charlotte found herself behind Arnold; her eyes were on his heavy, tight, white buttocks and she was presented with occasional glimpses of the back of his bouncing cock and balls as they all ascended a dimly gas-lit, thinly carpeted stairway, the wooden treads creaking. During the brief, steep climb she became keenly aware that the Count, close on her heels, must have been enjoying a fine view of her pussy lips lightly touching against one another as her buttocks wobbled.

Nothing in Charlotte's experience had prepared her for the amazing room into which she was led. The carpet, ceiling and one wall with its heavy curtains were deep purple. The wall with the door in it was mirrored, as was the inside of the door and one wall at right angles to it. On the fourth wall, covering it entirely, was a luridly pornographic mural, depicting dozens of naked men and women desporting themselves sexually in every conceivable manner, their genitals hideously exaggerated, the cocks so enormous that had they been real, they would have ripped apart the orifices they stuffed.

'Not quite Michelangelo,' muttered the Count as, closing the door, he saw Charlotte's eyes travelling in astonishment over the mural, 'but equally as pleasing.' The extraordinary room had the effect of almost stunning her. She stood very still; only her eyes moved, wandering from a brightly painted scene of a girl with two cocks in her mouth, one in her pussy, one in her arse and one in each hand, to the big bed in front of the mural – covered in purple satin and strewn with matching cushions – to a clumsy, black-painted wardrobe, coming to rest on a scarlet, padded contraption which appeared to be a cross between a dentist's chair and an operating table. The affair was positioned near to the corner where the mirrored walls met. It had a flat top, perhaps two feet square, on a heavy wooden frame, an extension of which sloped down steeply from one end to meet a padded step which was roughly the length of a shin bone. Threaded at several points through holes in the frame were heavy, black leather straps with large brass buckles.

Charlotte was given no time for her eyes to explore the room further. Gripping her elbow hard the Count said, 'I see you are fascinated by my bondage table, my dear Charlie. Well, it is to be all yours for just as long as we decide. And you are to be all – ours.' He grinned evilly. 'Is this not so, Jeremy?'

Jeremy, his doped gaze raking Charlotte's buttocks, grunted assent.

'Then shall we secure the young beauty right away so that she begins to accustom herself to her constraint?'

'Absolutely.' Jeremy moved forward to take her other arm and together the two took her, although her feet were reluctant to move, to the contraption. 'Kneel on the step and flatten yourself along the top,' he instructed her.

Charlotte's experience of being tied up was limited to one occasion. Jeremy had spreadeagled her naked on her bed and knotted her wrists and feet to the brass bedstead with silk scarves. He had teased her sexually for what had seemed like an interminable time, arousing her to unbearable heights and then, when she was begging for it with tears in her eyes he had fucked her; a fuck made in Heaven, he had promised her, and that was exactly what it had been. But this was something very different, sinister in its way.

Conscious of the rapid thumping of her heart, Charlotte did as asked, indenting the thickly padded step with her knees and stretching herself forward along the top. Her belly flesh shrank momentarily from the cold of the red leather, then relaxed. With her chin resting on the front edge of the table, she fleetingly noticed that she was facing her reflection in the corner where the wall mirrors met; this was then blocked by Arnold's plump, unstirring genitals as he moved in front of her. Swivelling her eyes first one way then the other she saw from side images that Jeremy and Alexis had dropped to their knees at her legs; Arnold sank down in front of her, his face level with hers. The three men went determinedly about their bizarre business.

The adjustable step was made higher then secured so that Charlotte's thighs were perfectly accommodated between it and the table top, after which she was strapped in place most firmly by the three men. The belts were buckled around her ankles, the backs of her knees, halfway up her thighs, her waist – where the bodice rucked up above the small of her back – and her wrists, elbow crooks and biceps, whilst her arms stretched down the front legs almost to the floor. When the job was done she was unable to move more than her toes, her fingers and her head. For moments she could see little because her hair had fallen all about her face and down to her elbows; Jeremy took care of this by bunching it at the nape of her neck and knotting his handkerchief around it.

'Comfortable?' asked Count Petrovski, standing back to admire her with a cynical smile.

The straps bit, the position was awkward; comfortable she was not. But little thrills of excitement were surging through her belly. She was overwhelmingly aware that, with her knees wide apart and her naked loins framed by black boots and a black bodice, her bottom hole and pussy were most crudely on show. In the mirrors, she watched all three pairs of male eyes feasting on her, and in particular on her private parts. She became filled with a desperate need for sexual contact, her pussy ached for it; only her bonds prevented her hands from flying between her legs.

The sight of the heavy leather straps cutting into Charlotte's soft white flesh, the knowledge that she was utterly helpless, the ultimate slave, filled Lord Brexford with raging lust. The sexual rules which applied to his wife did not apply to his mistress; Charlotte was fair game for anything. For his gratification she would be subjected to whatever he decided. His eyes strayed to Arnold. The lad might be a homo, but Lord Brexford saw that Charlotte's plight had inspired his short, fat dick to a certain amount of growth; filled with a sudden yearning to find out to what dimensions it might aspire, Jeremy went over to Arnold, draped an arm around his shoulder and walked him to the front of the table, positioning him with his groin inches from Charlotte's face.

'Get that up for us, Charlie,' he muttered thickly.

Only too happy to oblige, whilst Count Petrovski again put a match to his pipe of opium, Charlotte poked out her tongue, scooped it beneath Arnold's foreskin and lapped his cock into her mouth. Arnold shoved his hips forward until his shaved pubis touched her upper lip and his balls her chin.

The observation of how Charlotte's pussy lips gave a distinct twitch as she received the entire, rising dick in her mouth and of how her cheeks drew inwards as she avidly sucked served to aggravate Jeremy's lust. He hurriedly stripped off his jacket, kicked off his shoes and got out of his trousers and underpants; his freed cock stuck out and up, thick and solid through his shirt tails and the points of his tweed waistcoat. He fiercely fisted his hard-on, his eyes goatishly hooked on Charlotte's mouth job.

The sight, in a side mirror, of Jeremy's actions, caused Charlotte to suck with even more enthusiasm; within seconds Arnold's prick had achieved impressive dimensions which its flaccid state had belied, growing until she could accommodate only its huge glans and two inches or so. At least another six fine inches, wet with her saliva, were poled between her encircling lips and his groin. Longing, but frustratingly unable, to handle the heavy balls, Charlotte turned the attentions of her mouth on them instead. She drew first one, then the other, inside it, then slurped her tongue over the undersides of both of them whilst Arnold's dick was flattened all the way up the side of her face and probing her hair.

Aware that not only was she giving Arnold what was perhaps the mouth treat of his life – and, incidentally that the young man was by no means all homosexual – but that she was also greatly turning on the other two men by her lasciviousness, Charlotte became more and more inflamed; her toes and buttocks clenched, her fingers writhed, her pussy oozed.

Craving some mouth music himself, Jeremy moved in on Arnold to push him to one side and nudge his glans between Charlotte's sensuous lips. As she began to blow the familiar, well-loved penis her eyes wandered and she noticed, in the mirrors – her only means of visual communication with the rest of the room – two things; that Count Petrovski was getting out of his clothes and Jeremy's hand was resting on Arnold's buttock. What was obscured from Charlotte's view was the fact that Arnold's hand was also on Jeremy's behind, moving with it as he rocked his cock in her mouth.

The Count, naked, heavily endowed with body hair as black as that of his head, approached. 'My turn, I believe,' he muttered behind Jeremy, 'you are hogging the girl to yourselves.'

'A mouth as sweet as her fanny,' grunted Jeremy. 'Be my guest and welcome, Alexis.' He withdrew and stepped aside, making room for the Count between himself and Arnold.

Yet another eager cock found its way past Charlotte's equally eager lips, yet another size and shape and taste. She had become so horny she would gladly have received a regiment of pricks – she would happily have sucked off Frankenstein's monster. But the feeling she craved most – fingers, tongue, cock, candle, anything it could accommodate, in her wet and pleading pussy – was denied her.

Then Jeremy moved from the others to close in behind her, firmly gripping his hard-on, and for a moment she thought she was about to experience the penetration she needed. But he was there only to tease, to take full advantage of her bondage. He merely touched his cockhead on her bottom hole, worked it slowly down her perineum, jiggled it over her pussy lips and stepped back a pace, face a wanton mask as he masturbated, eyes piercing where cock was not about to enter. Charlotte groaned in frustration on her mouthful of turgid penis.

She noticed that Alexis's hand was far busier with Arnold's behind than Jeremy's had been; he was

squeezing a buttock and by the way a finger stabbed, she surmised that its tip must be inside
Arnold's bottom hole. Never having experienced at
first hand any such act before, Charlotte found that
it, and the implications of what might be about to
follow contrived, wickedly, to turn her on even further. The idea that she was about to witness one
man screwing another sent a massive tremble of
bawdiness through her. Her head bobbed frantically
as her tongue flicked greedily all around the leanly
aristocratic cock which she presumed was going to
perform the forbidden deed; meanwhile, she watched
it's owner's hand as, with mounting enthusiasm, it
rifled the musician-cum-ballet dancer's buttocks and
bottom hole.

But Alexis, as Jeremy on many occasions, liked to
string out his pleasures. He suddenly backed away
from Charlotte's face and unhanded Arnold's behind.
'A little more to smoke, no?' he suggested. 'Let us
take the evening's sport with agreeable slowness, the
more to savour it.' As he passed Jeremy on the way
to the table where he had left his pipe who was steadily fisting his cock he muttered, 'Surely you do not
intend to bring yourself off? So soon?'

Jeremy grinned sloppily, let go of himself and unbuttoned his waistcoat. 'Not I. Just to keep flying
steadily.'

'This will help you, my friend.' Alexis took fresh
opium from his jacket pocket, recharged the pipe, lit
it, inhaled and handed it to Jeremy who filled his
lungs with the sweet smoke before passing the pipe on
to Arnold. Jeremy then finished stripping naked.

Riding her tantalising and unserviced high, helplessly watching three naked, rampant males who were
each in their way splendidly endowed and lusting for

131

them all, Charlotte at least was not to be denied a share in their narcotic. Arnold placed the pipe between her lips. With her eyes latched beggingly on the fine genitalia which were inches from them she took a longer, deeper drag on the opium than before. As it was withdrawn from her mouth she craned her neck in an attempt to replace the pipe stem with Arnold's cock.

'No,' snapped Jeremy. Arnold moved out of reach. 'You can suffer just a little more, Charlie, whilst we finish our smoke. Then we shall all pleasure ourselves in your poor, panting pussy.'

They smoked in silence, offering her no more, their eyes constantly wandering over her need-engulfed loins which, because of the tight, restraining thigh and waist ropes had very little opportunity of movement. She could clench her buttocks. She was able to rock her hips very slightly, but nowhere near enough to get any sort of sensual enjoyment from the padded edge of the table. She suffered on until she saw in the mirror that the pipe was out and that the Count was laying it aside. No longer able to help herself she loudly moaned, 'Will someone now please, please fuck me?'

Raising a lecherous, amused, stoned eyebrow, Jeremy got up from where he had been perched on the edge of the purple bed. 'Who could refuse a plea of such eloquence?' he asked mockingly. 'We shall all fuck you, I have told you that. Who would you like to ram his prick home first – the Count, the Lord, or the ballet dancer?'

Her elocution training deserted her. 'I don't bleedin' care!'

Tutting and shaking his head, Jeremy went to her and crouched, his mouth close to her ear. 'It seems, then, that I must be wasting my money on you,' he hissed, appearing to be genuinely annoyed. 'Is my education in vain that you come up with such an answer in so ill-bred a manner?' He straightened up, taking his cock in his hand and rubbing the glans down her cheek. 'Now,' he rasped, 'I'll try once more. Who would you have fuck you first out of we three?' He raised his voice threateningly. 'Who?'

'You, of course, Jeremy My Lord,' she quietly responded, voice trembling, accent faultless.

'Better. Much better.'

Her eyes wandered, watching each of his three reflections as he got to his knees between hers on the step behind her. Then she let out a gasp of grateful relief as she felt his cock sliding all the way up her, filling her, until his springy pubic rug bumped into her buttocks. He hovered, then withdrew slowly to the glans and slammed it back into her.

As Jeremy proceeded to pump away in Charlotte with unbridled enthusiasm, Count Petrovski, seated close to Arnold on the bed, moved in on him. Taking hold of his huge cock he began to masturbate him. Arnold leaned back on his hands, his glazed eyes fixed on Jeremy's determined humping. Charlotte's head had started to roll around on the point of her chin; as she caught sight of Alexis's behaviour it went very still. The Count's fist was jumping up and down Arnold's machine more or less in time with Jeremy's fucking her. Discovering that the homosexual act added spice to her already severely inflamed lust, as Petrovski's head ducked to mouth the ballet dancer's cock, she found the spectacle overwhelmingly wanton; the combination of it and the prick pounding her pussy brought to her an orgasm so intense that she screamed.

Despite his relish Jeremy had no intention – yet –

of climaxing. With admirable restraint, as he felt Charlotte's vaginal walls pulsing, he forced himself to slide his prick out of her before her pussy's climactic actions brought him off. Noting the reflected direction of her glazed stare, he followed it. Alexis had raised his mouth from Arnold's hard-on at Charlotte's scream, yet his hand still gripped its base. Putting a foot down to the floor and standing up, Jeremy said, 'Arnold's turn at Charlie, no, Alexis? That is, before you two get so carried away with one another that it will be too late for me to fulfil my promise to her.'

'In my house it is never too late for anything.' The Count got to his feet, helped Arnold up by his elbow and lead him to the bondage table. 'Fuck her good and hard,' he said, as Arnold took Jeremy's place on his knees behind Charlotte, 'with all the energy that you would put into a vigorous dance.' One of Alexis's hands hooked and groped beneath the young man's buttocks as with the other he guided Arnold's cockhead between Charlotte's moist pussy lips. 'Give it to her as much as you please,' he muttered. 'You may come if you feel like it – I should rather enjoy having you fully relaxed when I bugger you.'

Arnold was readier to climax than the Count had imagined. His backside set to heaving feverishly, his thigh muscles standing out in hefty bands as if hewn from white marble as he went at Charlotte like a fully charged screwing machine, he banged away to bring her a second orgasm before rapidly coming himself. His hot seed hosed into her, but his final jerk caused him to draw back too far, his cock slipped out of her and the last drops of his sperm spurted over the backs of her thighs.

Clambering unsteadily from his perch, Arnold

stumbled to the bed where he collapsed as Petrovski closed in for his turn. The Count's thighs were too long for him to achieve his objective kneeling on the step, and he had not the patience to adjust it. Instead he began to fuck her standing, legs straddling Charlotte's calves, hands on her hips. Her eyes were closed. She was, for the moment at least, sated, hardly noticing that the slender cock which poled her was any different from its predecessor. Then she felt an insistent prodding at her lips and opened her eyes to see that the prick demanding entry there was Jeremy's and that the man now poking her was Count Petrovski. Her lover's dick crammed inside her mouth and within seconds, impaled at both ends, the remarkable Charlotte was greedily gobbling as her pussy became aroused yet again.

Like Jeremy before him, Alexis had no intention of spilling his semen in Charlotte; he was saving that event for Arnold's backside. Visited by a craving for a foretaste of bottom hole, his prick thoroughly lubricated by a mixture of Arnold's sperm and Charlotte's vaginal juices, he pulled out of her. Grasping her buttocks, his fingertips almost meeting in their cleft he stretched them apart and positioned his glans on her slightly opened, pinkish hole, and pushed.

Charlotte grunted with pain; the sound, muffled as it was by Lord Brexford's cock, might have been a moan of pleasure – as indeed it became moments later when the slender penis breached her sphincter.

It was the briefest of bum-humps. Jerking but a third of his cock inside Charlotte's bottom, the Count soon found himself approaching orgasm. With a pang of regret Charlotte felt him slip out of her. Her mouth fully occupied, she watched his reflection as he took his lanky, hairy, naked self to the bed where he raked smouldering eyes over the perfectly moulded behind of his AC/DC friend. Arnold was on his belly, one knee bent, his head cradled in his arms. Petrovski stooped, stretching out his hand.

Jeremy pulled his prick from Charlotte's lips. Crouching, he began to unfasten the straps of her arms, one eye on the bed. 'I don't allow men to do to me, any more, what Alexis is about to do with Arnold,' he muttered. He moved from her freed hands and arms to the belt around her waist and unbuckled it. 'Nevertheless, I love the sensation of it.' He started on her leg straps. 'So, I shall have you do it to me.'

She frowned, mystified, paying but vague attention to Alexis who, perched on the bed, was softly stroking Arnold's buttocks, Jeremy helped her up and off the bondage table. Cramped, sore, she stretched her muscles and rubbed the strap marks on her arms as Alexis left Arnold to open the door of the black painted wardrobe and take from it a tin of petroleum jelly.

'You have dildos in there, I recall?' asked Jeremy, joining him.

'Of a variety of shapes and sizes. Please help yourself,' said Alexis.

Confused and most horny from her short threesome which had ceased before she could come again, Charlotte silently watched as Alexis took his tin of jelly to Arnold and Jeremy brought her a dildo. He put the artificial penis in her hand. It was small, just over half the size of his hard-on, fashioned in pink rubber and well shaped, with nicely rounded balls and thin, velvet straps attached. He had her hold it, sticking out between her legs, like a man fisting himself while he ran two of the straps around her to tie them in a bow at the small of her back, and brought the third one from the balls and under her crotch to join it to the bow. Then he stood back with a smug and dirty grin as she let go of the dildo; her gaze wandered over three reflections of herself metamorphosed into some kinky, beautiful hermaphrodite, her pink erection standing straight forward, with curly red pubes lapping over its base, an effect somehow made the more lurid by the black velvet bodice and knee-length black boots.

Count Petrovski was busy with his jelly, lubricating Arnold's back passage. Jeremy joined him to scoop two fingerfuls from the tin and then returned to Charlotte, smearing the lubricant over the dildo. As she had previously been obliged to, he knelt on the bondage table, his groin backed off its edge to make room for his hard-on. Gruffly, he said, 'Do up the belts around my wrists and the backs of my knees.'

With her mind fighting to come to terms with the aberrant scenario, Charlotte fastened the buckles, shockingly aware at the same time that the Count was making ready, poising over Arnold's back, for penetration. She buckled the last strap with her eye on Alexis's buttocks as they became taut, trembled, and heaved, then, as Arnold grunted heavily, she was distracted by Jeremy's shaking voice telling her, 'Put it in. Put the thing in me. Take your time.'

Kneeling on the step, she pulled aside a buttock to open her lover's bottom hole, placed the smooth and greasy, nearly pointed rubber glans against it and gently pushed her hips forward, watching wide-eyed as the dildo began to sink in with less effort than she had expected. She stopped, scared to hurt him, but he urged her gratingly to keep going until it was all the way up him. When she could see nothing of the pink rubber prick, with her pubic thatch pressing against and sinking between Jeremy's buttocks, he gasped, 'Fuck me just like I fuck you. Fuck me and toss me off at the same time.'

Charlotte found herself in the freakiest weirdland that she had ever entered. Having no lesbian tendencies, she had never had occasion to use a dildo. Now she discovered something compellingly sensual about rocking her hips back and forth in the fashion of male copulation to bugger her lover whilst fisting his hot, throbbing cock. The base of the dildo jiggled arousingly on her clitoris, the thin velvet strap teased as it nestled tightly between her pussy lips. Her languid, half-stoned eyes moved raunchily around – from the dirty business directly below them, to the three reflections of her bum-fucking, and on to the single image of the homosexual activity taking place on the purple bed against the pornographic background of the mural. There they remained transfixed, for long moments, as her buttocks and wanking hand moved ceaselessly.

She had hardly dared even to imagine what homosexuals got up to with one another. She knew that for some reason such activity was an imprisonable offence; now, watching Count Petrovski's lusty buggery, and catching regular glimpses from the side of his long length of cock as it plunged up and down in Arnold's anus, she wondered why on earth why. The men, judging from their frequent grunts and panting breath, were in the clutches of as fierce emotions as was she. She enjoyed a cock up her bottom now and then – she just had – why should not they? It was only a variant of carnal love.

These thoughts drifted but vaguely and briefly through Charlotte's mind before being obliterated by the incredible tide of ribaldry which surged through her as, belly and pussy on fire, yet another climax began to take hold of her. Jeremy's loins, which had been rocking slightly back and forth against her own in counter-rhythm, went suddenly rigid. A low sound, pure rutting animal, escaped him. His cock appeared to swell to even greater dimensions in her hand as his balls eructed their warm, sticky fluid through it.

At the same time, the orgasm engulfing Charlotte caused her, just like a spunking male, to ram her artificial dick hard up Jeremy's arsehole and hold it all the way in there, her entire body trembling and shuddering as if she were actually shooting semen into his bowels. She collapsed forward across his back, buried in him, gasping along with his gasps.

When, minutes later, Charlotte's eyes flickered open, the deviant activity on the bed had reached its logical conclusion. Alexis faced the ceiling, one arm flung out across the back of Arnold's unmoving shoulders; both men appeared to be sleeping.

Charlotte felt utterly drained. At Jeremy's mumbled, barely intelligible request she straightened up, rocked backwards to unplug his bottom hole, then got off the step and wearily fumbled his straps undone. She wandered to the bed, dildo in place and wobbling, and crashed down on it next to Arnold.

Heaving himself off the bondage table, Jeremy turned around to sit on its edge, facing the bed. Charlotte's long black boots and long-sleeved black bodice had almost, in the low light, disappeared against the dark purple satin of the bedspread. In Jeremy's repletely foggy state she appeared to him as a disembodied white bottom and a pair of thighs. As he pondered the curious sight and studied the naked male bodies sprawled on the bed his mind, seldom sluggish for long, began once more to function clearly.

Count Petrovski, Jeremy mused, was greatly talented in his offbeat way. His was a sexually haunting presence; apart from being AC/DC and a refined expert in the complicated art of sado-masochism, he was also well versed in the occult. It occurred to Lord Brexford that it would be a splendid idea to have the Count stay at Deal Manor for two or three days. He could then play a major role in the degradation of Miss Claire Petty and in the further initiation of the delectable Ellie Branks.

He must remember to consult with the Count about arrangements for these most interesting events before taking his sated mistress back to Hyde Park Square and having one more good fuck with her before retiring for the night. Charlotte, he knew, would get exceptionally horny a little later – and many times in the future – on the memory of what she had witnessed and indulged in on this wildly licentious evening.

Chapter Nine

Ever since her raunchy experiences up at the manor Miss Petty had been in fearsome mood – or at least so it had seemed from the point of view of her girls. More bottoms had been caned during those days – and for the most trivial of reasons – than had been in the previous month. Poor Georgina's bared, fat behind had received a beating designed to preclude her sitting comfortably, if at all, for at least a week.

But in truth, the headmistress's disposition had nothing whatsoever to do with bloody-mindedness, foul temper or an early onset of the menopause – all possible reasons muttered darkly by her charges. Lord Brexford's treatment of her, and his promise of an invitation to an orgy had left her more randy than she had ever been before in her life, a stormy lust in need of slaking raged continuously in her loins, and the administration of merciless thrashings followed by solitary and furious masturbation was the only way of temporarily relieving her sexual craving – except for one notable incident, that is.

When the expected invitation to the manor on Saturday evening failed to materialise, Claire, desperate for satisfaction greater than that achieved by her own fingers, and yearning for a cock and balls and the rough touch of a male, sent a short note to her married lawyer and, occasional lover in Shingley Bay, begging him to visit her urgently at the school; it was a matter of life or death, she wrote.

It would almost certainly have been a matter of life or death had Gerald Crossfield's formidable spouse discovered the true reason for him leaving the house on Saturday evening – something he had never done before. She had long had nagging suspicions that there was a mistress somewhere, and had once observed Gerald talking intimately with Claire Petty in the village, and had judged her to be too pretty for the moral good of any comfortably married man.

The few girls who saw Gerald Crossfield emerge from his landau and pair outside Chalmers, in his smart overcoat and gloves and wearing a homburg, assumed he was either a parent or a member of the board of governors. The thought of Miss Petty having a lover was inconceivable, although in his early forties and with smart side whiskers, Crossfield was a fine looking man.

The lawyer had never before received a letter such as this from Claire Petty. He was quite convinced she was in some sort of serious trouble – which, indeed, she was, but hardly of the variety he was expecting.

When he rapped on the door of her study he was five minutes earlier than her note had suggested. Whilst waiting for her to bid him enter he heard a swish, a sharp slapping sound and a gasp, followed by low mutterings. He knocked again, louder. Seconds later there was the noise of a key turning in the lock and the door was opened by a slightly breathless Claire Petty. A tearful, pretty young girl, both hands clutching her buttocks, brushed past him and scurried off down the corridor. The headmistress asked him in and then, to his utmost surprise, locked the door behind them.

She was somewhat flushed, he noted. A lock of her normally neatly coiffured hair strayed down one cheek. She appeared extremely agitated. 'Why, Gerald,' she stuttered, 'you're, you're early.' Instead of greeting him with a kiss as he expected, she hurried to a high chair which was reversed to face into a corner, took a cane from its leather seat and hung it over her fireplace where heaped coals burned cheerfully.

Crossfield removed his homburg and gloves which he dropped in the hat and put upside down on a chair. As he unbuttoned his greatcoat he said, 'I gather you just caned that gel?'

'I did, yes.'

'An unfortunate but occasionally wholly necessary duty as I understand it.'

'Indeed.'

He hung the coat on a hook behind the door. 'Your letter was most compelling,' he told her. 'What is this crisis so urgent that you even lock the door?'

The urgent crisis, of course, was raging in Miss Petty's pussy, and she had timed the evening's thrashing to coincide with her lover's arrival so that she should be at her horniest for him. However, now that he stood before her in the flesh, all was not exactly as it had been in her imagination. He was concerned for her, and was not exhibiting any sexual interest. She felt an awkwardness she had not bargained for; the ache in her loins subsided slightly. But she had not anticipated the need to make up any excuses, and now it was too late to do so. Hesitantly she went to him, brushing the lock of hair from her pinkish cheek. She put her arms around him, pressed herself to him and kissed him on the lips. The response was uncertain. 'I've missed you so,' she told him.

'Yes. And I you.' He frowned. 'But that's hardly the point. Tell me what trouble you are in, Claire.'

Now that she had him in her arms, the desperate urge, brought to a pitch by the caning of yet another chubby, bared young bottom which she normally relieved with a good frigging, swept over her again. She rolled her groin wickedly against his. 'Woman trouble.'

He was still far from clear what was going on. 'Yes. But will you kindly explain? What woman?'

'This woman. I needed you. I need you, Gerald.' Somehow she could not prevent her next words spilling from her lips as she pulled his ear down to them. 'I need you and your nice big cock.'

His bushy eyebrows shot up. He pushed her away from him to arm's length, staring in astonishment at her. Seldom had she employed bad language during their sexual encounters, and never anything as frankly explicit as that. 'My God,' he breathed, 'such lewd talk. What on earth has got into you? And you mean you risked the suspicion of my wife, perhaps discovery even, by calling me away on a Saturday evening because you're feeling in the mood for sex? I find that most incredible.'

'Is it? Yes, I suppose it is. I'm sorry. But somehow I just had to, Gerald. Hell how I need you.'

His momentary irritation passed. He wanted to be angry, but faced with his attractive mistress in a flushed and horny state – his only fantasy in what was largely a grey and regimented world – he could not. But he was flustered, a touch embarrassed even, by her flagrancy.

'Kiss me, my darling, oh kiss me,' she entreated, forcing herself close to him once more, crushing her lips against his and thrusting her tongue into his mouth, but inciting from him only a weak reaction as she ground her pubis against his.

As her hand found its way to his genitals and squeezed, his groin wanted to cringe away. He was totally unused to such ribald behaviour from her – or from any other woman. Their love-making was always carrried out between the sheets in the room of a small country hotel, having undressed discreetly. Now, to his amazement and growing alarm, she slid down his body to her knees and began undoing his fly with impatient, clumsy fingers whilst muttering, 'I want it, I want it, I need it.' It was as if some sex fiend had got into her – which it had. He felt completely out of his depth with her, like finding himself in the wrong court giving evidence in the wrong case. His instinct was to turn and run but he was too frozen by her actions to do so – and by the time the paralysis had passed, he was unable to, because his trousers were halfway down his thighs and his underpants on their way to join them.

Claire had never fellated Gerald Crossfield, although she had had some limited experience in the matter with one or two previous gentlemen, including Lord Brexford. Gerald had never encouraged or even hinted at the act – to which he was in fact a stranger – and she, the demure schoolmistress, playing the part of one slightly shameful at their adulterous relationship, had therefore not performed it with him. There was no stopping her now.

Stunned, the lawyer gazed down as his flaccid penis disappeared entirely inside Claire Petty's mouth. She sucked on it like a hungry baby on a thumb, whilst with one hand she grasped his balls and with the other clutched and squeezed his buttocks. So shocked by this was he that he was barely able to move; he even experienced a pang of revulsion. He thought she must have gone raving mad.

That was at first. Then, when Crossfield was trying to make up his mind how to put an end to this madness, his libido, almost inevitably, began gradually to take him over. It was with agreeable surprise that, without any conscious effort on his part – to the contrary even – he discovered, as his penis began to rise, that his aversion had vanished.

Moments later, Claire was slurping, licking and sucking on a cock gone so hard that her mouth could accommodate only one-third of it; and Gerald Crossfield had miraculously gone the way of all heterosexual men with their prick between female lips. He was grunting and gasping and rocking his hips, experiencing a salacious joy he would never have believed possible.

Having got him up and overcome all resistance, Claire now craved to have that turgid hunk of meat where her fingers would have been at that moment had Gerald failed to arrive. Getting to her feet, eyes shining, lips drooling, she literally ripped off her clothes, tearing three buttons from her bodice and two from her skirt as she did so, accidentally pulling apart a seam in her cotton knickers. She led the wordless lawyer, whose amazement was now but a background to his aroused lust, to her punishment chair and spun it around. Sitting him where the hands of her latest victim had so recently rested, naked but for her flat shoes and a string of large, round, green beads, she straddled him, facing him, her feet on the floor. Fisting his cock, she positioned her desperate pussy over it and sank down.

She fucked him – and how she fucked him. He never had a chance to move, not that he had the slightest need or desire to. He sat there mesmerised, trousers and pants bunched around his ankles, tie and jacket and waistcoat neatly in place, as his Rubens-plump mistress bounced herself, braced on her arms, hands flat on his knees behind her, up and down on his cock. Her hair worked itself loose, and more and more wisps and locks began to stray over her face and neck; all her pleasing excess of white flesh trembled and shook and her buxom tits with their erect, pink nipples were flung from side to side and up and down as if possessed with life of their own, whilst her beads tossed around like a string of cork floats on a choppy sea.

Gerald Crossfield watched and experienced in ribald wonderment. Never had it been like this for him with any woman, and here was his strict and respectable headmistress gone wild as the legendary Messalina. As his eyes slid up and down, from flying tits to riding pussy, his mouth slowly slackened; his slender hands never once left the edges of the chair.

This was a screw, as far as Claire was concerned, with but one, most urgent objective. There was no question of prolonging the pleasure – she had to come. And come she did, after but a few minutes of sexual exertion so violent it caused rivulets of sweat to run between her tits and trickle down her belly. She came with a huge bellow of relief, her pussy going through maddening contractions on Gerald's cock, dragging the sperm from him in great bursts.

She sagged forward into him, sweaty cheek flopping onto his shoulder, panting and gasping as if she had just finished a four minute mile, her pumping, galloping heartbeat reaching his chest all the way through her tits and his clothing as he sat, position unchanged, eyes closed, cock oozing, vaguely aware of the sperm which spread over the tops of his thighs as it ran out of her vagina.

An insistent rapping on the door served to bring them out of their après-sex lethargy. 'Was everything all right?' matron wanted to know, having been alerted to the headmistress's climactic shout by one of the girls. Indeed, it was. It was. As matron's heels clicked busily off down the wooden corridor, Claire Petty climbed from her now wilted cock with the laziest of beatific smiles.

'My God,' mumbled Gerald. 'My God, my God. My God.'

Jeremy Brexford, fresh back from London, having elected to steal a peep at Chalmers that evening through his telescope, happened to have witnessed all the scandalous goings on in Claire Petty's study, starting with the caning of the unfortunate girl. He finally rested his overtaxed eye.

'My God,' Jeremy muttered to himself.

Several days passed, during which Miss Petty, fearful of her excesses bringing about a scandal, restricted her canings to one only. On the following Thursday, she finally received her invitation to Deal Manor – for Friday evening rather than the expected Saturday. It came by way of a brief note from Lord Brexford, delivered by hand in an envelope and bearing a wax seal with his family coat of arms stamped into it. It read: 'You are expected tomorrow evening for supper and all that is to follow. Kindly make your own way here.' It was signed, simply, 'Brexford'.

Friday was the longest day of Miss Petty's life. Anybody who crossed her path found her vague and distracted, fumbling over even the simplest of questions; her mind was crammed with prurient speculation about the forbidden delights awaiting her up on the hill. An orgy, she had been promised. The words 'all that is to follow' kept repeating themselves in her head the whole day through.

She chose to run herself up in the pony and trap, and not to have the caretaker take her. But as soon as she was within the private wood she began to wish that she had not gone alone, for although there was no rain it was a dark, windy evening of heavy cloud, so black that she could barely make out the shape of the pony in front of her. The trees pressed menacingly in on both sides, wind howling and whistling through them, branches creaking, leaves and twigs flying, and, stout-hearted though she was, the formidable head-mistress found herself attacked by twinges of fear.

Enormously relieved to emerge from the wood and to be on the sweeping drive of the house, she still experienced difficulty seeing her way. The manor itself was hardly visible up ahead, the dimmest of light coming only from one ground-floor window. She pulled the trap up at the foot of the broad flight of worn stone steps which led to the front doors and firmly braked the wheels so that the pony would not go wandering off. Getting down, she expected some-one to greet her for a chink of light appeared between the doors as one of them was slightly opened. But when she reached it, it had not moved any more.

The heavy door creaked as she pushed it open just enough to allow her through. Puzzled to find no one on the other side she closed it, her back to it, eyes raking the cold great hall with its flagstone floor and huge, granite arches. Although fitted with gas lights, it was dimly illuminated with just a few candles – full of black, threatening shadows with flickering edges. From somewhere at its far end came the sound of music, Vivaldi's Four Seasons, faint and echoey. Miss Petty made her hesitant way towards its source, the high heels of her boots ringing against the stone floor as she slowly moved forward with her heart in her mouth, almost as nervous as she had been in the wood.

Apart from the candles there was one other source of light; it trickled through a door which was ajar and from behind which came the music. Reaching this door, preparing to step gingerly through it, Miss Petty paused on the threshold of the room beyond in astonishment. She found herself in a banquet hall, high ceilinged and dominated by a huge oaken table. Despite its size it was pleasantly warm after the clammy chill of the hall; in massive fireplaces on walls facing one another, huge fires blazed. Three silver chandeliers, host to dozens of candles, hung low over the table. The only other light apart from that from the fires came from a chandelier above the heads of a string quartet playing in a corner.

The table could comfortably seat fifty, but there were only five people at it, gathered on either side of a sumptuously laid end. Lord Brexford, in tails, facing his wife at the top, who looked up to stare silently at Claire as she entered, was the only person she recognised.

Conversation ceased completely and at once. The other four turned their faces curiously towards her as a butler appeared from nowhere to relieve Claire of cloak and gloves. She was dressed in her very best black satin evening gown, all flares and flounces and with a low cut top showing to full effect her bosom on which lay three rows of pearls. The musicians played on. Nobody greeted her and the men failed to rise. She began to walk uncertainly towards them, a weak smile hovering around her mouth. Still not one word was spoken – but five pairs of eyes roved over her in what seemed to be mocking amusement. Unnerved, her steps faltered and she stopped yards from the table.

Lord Brexford hooked an imperious finger, summoning her forward. As she neared him, he waved a hand elegantly, like a flunky ushering someone into a room, at the vacant seat at the head of the table. The strange and silent non-greeting struck her dumb. Without a word she gathered her skirts and sat down, dreadfully embarrassed, avoiding all prying, probing eyes.

A servant slipped out of the shadows to her place to fill an emerald encrusted, silver goblet almost to the brim with red wine. Raising his own, Jeremy indicated that Claire should follow suit. When she did, he touched his goblet against hers then sipped the fine claret, watching her steadily over the rim. Desperate for some Dutch courage, she downed a copious draft; it warmed her fluttering belly as soon as it hit. The weird, silent staring carried on, filling her with agitation.

At last Jeremy spoke, his words falling devastatingly on her shamed and outraged ears, turning them as pink as the cheeks of one of her blushing girls. 'So,' he said, addressing the table, waving his goblet towards her, 'at last arrives the corrupt and scandalous woman we are all awaiting. Her name is Claire Petty; she is the supposedly respectable headmistress of Chalmers, the renowned finishing school for daughters of the rich and titled. But respectable she is not. Disreputable, she certainly is. Miss Petty' – he paused, eyes laughing cruelly at her – 'takes the most sordid pleasure from caning her charges on bared behinds and from frigging herself when it is done because the administration of punishment serves to inflame her lust.' He paused again. 'What is more she delights in giving the most lascivious gamahuche.'

Miss Petty gasped. She felt as if she were about to choke. Shakily she poured wine down her throat, spilling a little of it onto her breast. 'How dare you? How ... dare ... you ...?' she spluttered.

'Why Claire, you surprise me.' He raised a mocking eyebrow. 'Did I not promise to make you the star of an orgy? As I recall, you were indecently eager to adopt such a role. Surely the secondary actors and actresses should have some insight into the inner qualities of their star before the production begins, should they not?'

'But I, I ... you treat me like, like a piece of dirt in front of these people with whom I am not even acquainted. I repeat – how dare you, sir?'

'You will shortly get to know these good friends of mine, and my wife, most intimately – that is if you elect to stay. Before you make up your mind, I must warn you that you are to be degraded here to the utmost of our collective ability. You are to be shamed most thoroughly. You are to be severely beaten.'

She started to rise. 'I really don't think I ...'

'However,' he interrupted, 'I imagine that during the course of the evening your fanny will subject you to sensations unexperienced even in your wildest dreams – because I know you, Claire Petty. Through our one meeting and my telescope I already know you very well. You are a brazen, meretricious, shameless woman, a defiler of daughters of men of quality, and as such will you be treated. In short, amongst the orgiastic company in which you find yourself tonight, you *are* a star.' He grinned derisively. 'Will you leave us now, or will you stay to face up to your degradation?'

She sank back onto her seat, wriggling uncomfortably, eyes lowered, catching her confused reflection in the empty silver plate before her; her mind was in a turmoil. 'You have placed me in a most compromising position, Lord Brexford,' she muttered.

'Have I not?' He grabbed her elbow, fierceness in his grip. 'Look at me, damn you.'

She slowly raised her eyes to his. Humiliated as she felt, she was nevertheless impressed with the hauntingly sexual expression she read there as they stabbed hers, a look which seemed to demand she recall the episode together with he and the parlour maid, and after. That, and the combination of his burning fingers, contrived to make her feel helplessly weak, a schoolmarm reduced to cringing pupil.

'Well? Your answer. Do you stay – or do you go?'

'I . . . I . . . I . . .' Her mind raced, considering the bald alternatives. 'I stay.'

'I never doubted it.' He relaxed his hold on her to clap his hands, and two serving wenches appeared with bowls of steaming consommé with which to begin the meal. The mask of silence dropped as Jeremy introduced the others. Sophronia, in a svelte, golden gown, beamed innocent radiance at her as she took her hand, whilst the near satanic Count Petrovski curled his lips in a smiled salutation which appeared more like a sneer. The other two, a tubby, balding man with restless, red-veined eyes and heavy lips, and a slight, pretty young lady with coal black, perfectly straight hair and pleasingly high cheekbones were Aubrey Taff, a prominent Irish racehorse owner and breeder, and his latest in a formidable string of mis-

153

tresses, Jocelyn. Despite his rather unappetising apperance, Aubrey was a noted libertine.

The vestiges of normality which descended on the company lasted only until the soup plates had been cleared away. As the servants began to slice and serve tender flesh from one of a pair of roast suckling pigs, every eye once again fell on Claire as Jeremy said loudly, a tone of authority in his voice, 'You will now please remove your clothing, Miss Petty.'

She stared at him in disbelief. Her chin wobbled. 'I beg your pardon?' she responded weakly.

'Come now – are you gone suddenly deaf?' Lord Brexford crooked a finger at the shadows and a butler walked to the side of her chair. 'Stand up, take off your clothes, and give them to my man.'

'This is monstrous. It's . . .'

'Immediately. Or leave – immediately. Ah, but I forgot, you already made your decision. You stay.'

Miss Petty gulped down more wine, emptying her goblet, feeling the alcohol rush from her stomach to a head already gone dizzy from the effect of Jeremy's words. In a daze, she somehow managed to steel herself for the coming, terrible ordeal. She rose unsteadily to her feet, supporting herself with a hand on the table. She hovered there uncertainly while the quartet played the opening bars of 'The Four Seasons' summer music, until Jeremy ordered tersely: 'Get on with it, woman. What the hell are you waiting, for?'

Feeling that she was experiencing some awful dream, whilst the butler fixed his gaze on a chandelier, she reached behind her and unbuttoned her dress from neck to waist. Shrugging out of the shoulders, she pulled them and the sleeves down over her arms and off, reversing the sleeves in the process and revealing a plain white chemise. Looking anywhere but at her companions, she eased the dress down over her hips and stepped out of it. The butler, who seemed to have eyes in the back of his head, whilst still staring at the chandelier, held out his hand and she put the dress into it.

Claire hesitated once more, already feeling dreadfully exposed, until Jeremy said huffily, 'Come now, do not keep us waiting.' They were all eating, Claire's plate was filled. Crossing her hands in front of her on its hem, she pulled the chemise up and over her head; there was a sigh from Jeremy accompanied by a grunt from Alexis as her fat white breasts fell free, wobbling, with the three rows of pearls trembling over them. Miss Petty draped the chemise over the statue-like butler's extended arm and shifted her feet uncomfortably. With the sure knowledge that sex was to be the evening's main objective she had dressed accordingly and was wearing frilly, black lace, French knickers and sheer silk stockings with white garters. But she had certainly not anticipated being obliged to reveal these items until she had been coaxed into the right mood; this forced exposure at a decidely inappropriate time was a hideous embarrassment. Covering her breasts with her forearms, she made as if to sit down.

'Good God, woman, undress, I said,' stormed Lord Brexford through a mouthful of pork. 'Everything – the drawers, the stockings, the boots, everything. You may keep on your pearls and that is all.'

Nightmarishly trapped in this Gothic banqueting hall with the eyes of servants and musicians alike joining those of the distinguished company, as she removed first her boots, then her garters and stockings, Claire Petty felt as if she herself were the feast. Leaving the items strewn on the carpet – from where the butler retrieved them – she hooked her thumbs in the sides of her knickers and, firmly closing her eyes as if that would obscure her nakedness from everyone else as well, swiftly stripped them off.

'Give the drawers to me,' commanded Jeremy, stretching out his hand and, without looking, she handed them over. To guffaws and giggles from the others, he arranged them over the head of the uncut pig, crotch between its ears and over its snout, leg-holes draped on either side of its face. 'Suckling pig turned sucking pig,' he joked, making Sephronia hoot with laughter.

Again, Claire attempted to sit down, to put her pussy at least more or less out of view; again, Lord Brexford prevented her. 'We shall all now admire your ample and luscious curves more closely,' he told her. 'Before being allowed to get on with your meal, you will parade slowly around the table, across to the band and back.'

She reopened her eyes, trying not to focus on any-thing. Taking perhaps the deepest breath of her life she began to walk, with a hand and forearm over her tits and a hand covering her pussy. Impatiently, Jere-my said. 'That will not do at all, Miss Petty. Link your hands behind your neck.'

Well, she told herself, she was now in, way, way out of her depth – so she had better learn to swim. She did his bidding bravely, her breasts pulled up-wards and appearing the more shapely for it – not that she managed to give that fact any thought. All the way around the fifty seater table she marched, and across to the string quartet who played on as if nothing untoward were happening, then she returned to her chair, by far the longest journey of her life. Yet by the end of her nude trip the unexpected had occurred; her embarrassment fractionally subsided. Naked, she was assuring herself, was only that and no more, a perfectly natural state, and her body, albeit on the plump side and pushing forty, was smooth and agreeably attractive.

But still Lord Brexford would not allow her to sit down. He insisted that she stand on her chair and let down her chestnut hair from a coiffure which had taken her an hour to get right. Worse, as she did this, he rudely poked at her heavy pubic thatch with a forkful of pork.

Embarrassment returned with a vengeance. Miss Petty stared at her tormentor with shocked and bewildered eyes as he ran the small lump of meat down through her bush and between her chubby thigh tops to her pussy lips, rubbing it there. 'A nice and juicy cunt, my friends,' he announced. 'A fat, lust-filled little rabbit. I suggest that we all have a taste – for surely it will improve the flavour of the pork.' He popped the meat in his mouth and chewed with relish. 'Come, each one of you,' he said as he did this, 'a forkful of the most succulent. The belly of the pig sweetened with the sauce of the underbelly of the ...' Jeremy's cynical gaze roved over Claire's curves as he thought for seconds. '... of the flagellating masturbator,' he finished.

One by one they solemnly handed him a skewered piece of pork, and one by one they ate it after he had dipped it at her pussy lips. Only then, feeling abased and almost unbearably humiliated, was Claire permitted to take her seat.

She began miserably to toy with her food, lacking even the slightest appetite. She would have found it impossible, she knew, to swallow even the tiniest morsel, so she put nothing in her mouth.

The taunting began.

With the sweetest, friendliest of smiles, after swallowing a mouthful of food and washing it down with claret, Sophronia asked, sounding seriously interested as if she were perhaps questioning Miss Petty about a technical aspect of schooling, 'Tell us, Claire – what is it you find so fascinating about the naked bottoms of young girls? It is perhaps the texture, the shape? What is it?'

The headmistress stared fixedly, stonily at her plate of untouched food, feeling as if she were one of her charges up before her for punishment, being asked what she had been doing with her hand in the cookie jar.

Sophronia's smile turned wicked. She overloudly addressed the table in general. 'Miss Petty has the most extraordinary affinity for unclad posteriors. Apparently for the feeblest of reasons she will summon a poor girl to her study where she has her bend over a high chair, then raises her skirt, drops her drawers and canes her buttocks with the utmost of vigour. After which . . .'

Jeremy stopped her. 'Wait,' he said, 'let us hear it from her own sluttish lips. What is it you do then, Claire? What do you get up to when the beaten girl has departed?'

From somewhere she found the courage to glare at him. 'You already told them once, I believe.'

'And now I am telling them again. Or, rather, you shall. They will enjoy hearing it from you. What was it I watched you do to yourself through my telescope after Ellie Branks had been thrashed?'

'No.'

'*No?*'

'Come on, Claire, do tell us,' said Aubrey, jocularly, raking a jaundiced eye over her tits. 'Nothing to be shy about. Jocelyn gets up to that sort of thing most frequently, don't you Josie?'

The girl smirked prettily. 'No more than once or twice a day, darling. That is to say, if you mean what I believe you do.'

'Tell us,' grated Jeremy. 'Bloody well tell us – now.' There was an edge to his voice contrived to menace.

Claire's lips remained stubbornly sealed, though, remarkably, the situation was beginning to feel fractionally more bearable to her. She was trying to get accustomed to the idea that all that was happening to her was no more than an elaborate game. Perverse, surely, but a game nevertheless. Her nudity had almost ceased to bother her; bit by bit she was starting to feel the sexual tension around the table, even to appreciate the fact that she was the centre of attention.

'So,' spat Jeremy. He scraped his chair back from the table, jumped to his feet and plucked a burning candle from a chandelier above his head. Looming over Claire he held it inches from her nose. 'Hot wax on your nipples unless you answer my question immediately.'

She flinched away. 'You would not dare.'

'Are you sure?'

Count Petrovski got to his feet to take the candle from Jeremy. 'He would, but it's a speciality of mine. I'll do it.'

He exactly fitted the part of the sadist, she had already noticed that. But still she braved, 'And neither would you.'

'Ha!' The Count tipped the candle without delay or warning. She had no time to raise a hand. Wax dripped from the candle to blob, white as her flesh, on her breast close to a nipple.

Miss Petty gasped, grabbing at the place, though in fact it was the shock of his action rather than the pain – there was merely a slight burning sensation which immediately faded away – which caused her to blurt out what they were all waiting to hear. 'I masturbated.'

'You masturbated,' repeated Jeremy in satisfaction. He took the candle from Alexis and fitted it back in its place as the Count sat down. 'Innocent young girls are obliged to get their arses tanned black and blue by you to turn you on, so that you may enjoy a hearty wank.' He glanced around at the others. 'Let us all contemplate that revelation for a few moments.'

He resumed his place, cleared the last scrap of food from his plate and slowly chewed, a steely eye on Claire all the while. She peeled the dried wax from her breast, studiously avoiding the collective, searching glance.

Aubrey broke the silence. 'I suppose,' he said slowly, 'given my vast experience, if I had to categorise Miss Petty I would say she was an inventively wicked woman.' His red-veined eyes searched her face. They were unhealthily amused. 'If the parents should discover such a scabrous fact, their vengeance would, I imagine, be most severe.'

'But as we know, they have not,' observed Jeremy. 'It therefore falls upon us here to execute poetic justice on their behalf.' He clapped his hands and the plates were whisked away to be replaced by a dessert of fruit salad and strawberry mousse as the quartet began to play the winter, and final section, of 'The Four Seasons'. As the others ate, Claire decided that the only way she was ever going to get her head into this wantonly complicated sex game was to lighten it. She swallowed down a goblet of claret as if slaking a thirst with a glass of water; it was straight away replenished and she downed some more.

'Our pillar of society is now set on getting pixilated,' observed Sophronia. 'Should we allow that, Jeremy dear heart?'

'It will do no harm – provided that is, that she doesn't overdo it and pass out.' He paused. 'One more cupful Claire, and then perhaps you will be good enough to lie on the table and show us how you like to frig yourself.' The words slipped past Jeremy's lips as casually as if he had been suggesting that she show them her knitting, thus having the effect of cutting into Claire more deeply than anything previously said. A spasm of trepidation hit her belly; her pussy twitched.

'And the lady also likes to gamahuche, eh?' asked Aubrey through a mouthful of mousse. 'Get a thrill from sucking fellers off, do ya?'

Defiance now from the headmistress as the wine began to take effect. 'So what if I do?' she challenged with a toss of her head which bounced her loose hair over her bare shoulders.

Jeremy raised an eyebrow. 'Our star suddenly becomes irascible,' he commented as yet more wine disappeared down Claire's throat. He stayed her drinking hand. 'Enough of that, for the time being.' He raised his chin towards the unlaid table beyond the group, which stretched off across the room and stood, taking her by the elbow. 'Up you get, there, on your back.'

Claire found her kneecaps trembling as Jeremy led her to the spot and had her clamber up and onto her back at the table's centre with the grubby soles of her feet almost touching the beginning of the laid section. Her head spun and she closed her eyes as the lord began to arrange her how he wanted her. Compliant as a lump of plasticine, resigned, becoming accustomed to, even beginning to take sordid pleasure in, her predicament, she allowed her feet to be parted and shoved back towards her buttocks so that her knees were raised high. Her very first sexual stirrings of the evening began as she felt Jeremy's hands sliding over the plumpness of her belly and sampling her flesh. His fingers brushed down through her heavy bush, found her pussy lips and parted them.

'Our star's cunt in all it's naked glory,' he gloated. 'Feast your eyes, my friends.'

As the band played on and the servants, as they were obliged, went about their duties at table as if nothing of a ribald nature was taking place, Aubrey Taff leaned down the table, stretched out a hand with a silver dessertspoon of strawberry mousse with a cherry upon it, slipped the spoon between Jeremy's fingers and the gaping vulva, worked it a short way inside, then withdrew it and put it into his mouth, cleaning it. 'Delicious!' he proclaimed and his girl-friend giggled.

Delicious this scandalous behaviour was now becoming for Claire. This ultimate exposure and the intimate touch of Jeremy's fingers did the trick of turning her on; they all saw how her loins contracted in pleasure as the spoon was withdrawn. 'Open your eyes, Miss Coarse and Vulgar Petty, Miss Petty Wanker,' grunted Lord Brexford, his hands working their way up to her tits and fondling them.

She did so, taking seconds to focus properly on the candelabra over her head, no longer outraged by his words; ready. He pinched her nipples, hard, simultaneously, then let them go and reached up first for one candle, then another, nodding at Count Petrovski who left his seat to face him on the other side of Claire. He gave a candle to the Count, then plucked Claire's right hand from the table and put it over her pussy. 'Show them how very much you enjoy doing it, Miss Wanker,' he hissed. 'Frig yourself to orgasm while we give your tits a wax coating.'

'You're not going to hurt me too much?' mumbled Claire, not sounding very fearful as a finger found its way into her pussy up to the first knuckle and jerked.

'In the mind only, it hurts. The idea hurts. The pain, as you have already experienced, is minimal.' Jeremy glanced theatrically around the table. 'The show, and our star, hots up.'

The men each tipped their candle over her tits. Wax began to fall steadily, splashing over her big nipples and their surrounds, tingly, stinging, pleasantly burning. Happily woozy from the claret, now feeling not besmirched and assaulted but wonderfully debauched, Claire began to go wild. A second finger joined the one in her pussy and together they slid all the way up inside her to begin a frenzied jiggling. The tips of the fingers of her other hand and the ball of its thumb surrounded her clitoris area, squeezing and pinching. Her toes curled. Her legs began partly to close and open in regular, orgiastic movements, thighs banging and shaking, chubby inner flesh enveloping her busy hands as her rocking bottom caused her belly to tremble. And the wax dripped ceaselessly down to coat her nipples and an ever increasing area of their surrounds.

It was a masturbation display worthy of the most accomplished porn star and even more salacious because it was genuine. From aggrieved, debased, craven victim, Claire Petty had miraculously changed to a brazen hussy bringing herself off in public with an

163

abandon which left no member of the company un-aroused. In the less than three minutes it took for her to climax, there were two more wet pussies at the table and three cocks straining to be free of their enclosing evening trousers. As she came, Claire's big buttocks raised clear of the table top and slammed back down on it, one, two, three times. She whimpered and mewled; her fingers stilled.

'My God,' muttered Sophronia, eyes shining, thighs tightly squeezed together, 'so now we know a little more of the truth about the prim, finishing school headmistress. Amazing.'

Miss Petty's legs straightened slowly, her feet pushing aside cutlery, plates and cruet. Both hands remained, relaxed, at their post, the tips of two fingers loose inside her. Her nipples had disappeared beneath the soft coating of wax, and her tits looked like those in an air-brushed censored photograph, lumpy-white and unreal.

There was a limit to the activities which Lord Brexford would allow to take place in front of staff. As far as he was concerned, what had transpired so far was little more than a very risqué floor show. But now, with his cock craving release and his eyes sexually contemplating the delightful Jocelyn – whose titillated condition he had rightly deduced – he dismissed all the servants and the string quartet.

The music seemed more noticeable by its sudden absence. For long moments during which nobody found anything to say, the only sounds to relieve the silence were the crackling and spitting of the two fires and the intermittent howl of the wind as it whistled around the ancient house. Then Jeremy approached Jocelyn from behind to put his hands caressingly on her bared shoulders. 'Time for the evening to warm up thoroughly,' he said. 'May I sport a little with your delightful lady friend, Aubrey?'

'By all means – be my guest. It is what the saucy gel was born for. And Sophronia . . .?' There was a hesitant question in Aubrey's voice. This was his first visit to Deal Manor and he had never before met its mistress, though he had frollicked at orgies in London with Jeremy on two occasions.

'My pleasure,' Jeremy responded, as his flattened hands slid down the inside of Jocelyn's maroon taffeta *décolleté* to cup her bare breasts, 'You and my wife may of course . . . indulge.'

Sophronia would have preferred the indulgence to be with Count Petrovski, whom she found rather thrilling. She saw nothing much to attract her in the overweight and balding Aubrey Taff, but his hand was already crawling beneath her voluminous skirts and she was in any case moist between her legs.

The Count had other, more specialised, games in view. 'Where is it that you left the rope, Jeremy?' he asked, eyes roaming the room.

'Over there, on the dresser,' he told him as he dragged Joceyln's bodice down to expose a smallish, creamy pair of tits with tiny, hard pink nipples. He pulled the girl's chair around and away from the table, and cupped a hand under each breast. 'I confess an urge to rub my dick between these peaches,' he said.

She cracked a dimpled, lascivious smile, eyes almost as black as her hair burning brightly at the bulge in his trousers. 'And I confess an urge to roll my peaches around your,' she paused, reaching for a fly button, '. . . thing,' she finished.

As Jocelyn released Lord Brexford's pole, and Aubrey's fleshy lips – more agreeable than she had

165

expected – clashed with Sophronia's, while his fingers wormed their way under her knickers to find her damp cunt, Count Petrovski brought a large, coiled length of thin, white, silken rope to where Claire lay on the table, her eyes remaining closed and her hands on her pussy. He laid the rope down near her head and reached for one of her tits, digging long, finely polished and manicured fingernails under an edge of wax. With a start she opened her eyes.

'I believe that the erotic will be better served if we again see your nipples,' he murmured, as he began to strip off the wax. 'As I recall, they are blessed with large and dark coronas.' Claire silently looked on, fascinated, as candle wax and breast flesh parted company with ease. Her tits, of which she became physically aware once again for the first time since her overpowering orgasm only now, glowed with a pleasant warmth and stung very slightly. They were, she saw, interestingly flushed the palest of pink from their ordeal. As the last of the wax was stripped off, she raised and turned her head to observe with a moment's shock that Jeremy was standing in front of the seated Jocelyn with hips arched and trouser front gaping, whilst she was leaning into him to cushion her bared breasts around his big cock.

Miss Petty's head rolled and her gaze shifted across the table to alight but briefly on Sophronia and Aubrey, kissing and sexually fumbling, before her attention was drawn sharply back by the touch of a rope on her cheek. Alexis Petrovski had in his hand the coil of rope, and in his eye was a wickedly lecherous glint. 'I understand from Lord Brexford that you have begged for him to . . . beat you?' he asked.

Claire licked her lips. Perfectly relaxed now, in her nakedness, and content after her climax, she realised that she was beginning to revel in this dirty evening. Her head was still rather mussy but her words were steady as she boldly replied, 'I did not beg, sir. I merely asked.'

'You are the masochist then, as well as the sadist?'

'What I should like to be, but have never had much opportunity, is all things to all men.'

'I see. And women?'

She thought about it, as a picture of Georgina going down on Ellie Branks came clearly into her mind. 'Yes.'

'Then you are now amongst the right company. And, as you may have gathered, we have discussed in advance certain things which are to be done to our star. We had agreed that once you had been persuaded to – how do you say, toss yourself off? – you should then be restrained from performing such an act again. It is up to me now to tie you up – I trust you will offer no resistance?' His eyes shifted. He took note of Jeremy's buttocks humping back and forth as he tit-fucked Aubrey's girlfriend. He ogled the gropings of Sophronia and Aubrey then looked back at Claire. 'It would be a great shame to have to disturb my friends in order to have them hold you down.' He uncoiled the long rope in a heap on the table and found its centre.

Never having experienced it before, the idea of bondage scared Claire a little, but it also intrigued her. 'Please do with me as you will,' she told him with a defiant jut of her chin, but without the faintest notion of what she was letting herself in for – in fact, one of the perverted Count's favourite specialities.

'Sit up,' he said brusquely. When she had done so, he took hold of the side of her knee and moved her around so that her calves dangled over the edge of the table. He passed the central section of the rope over her head to her back, and looped it under her armpits to knot it beneath her breasts. Then he began winding each end most tightly around her, criss-crossing the rope between and around each breast until they were crushed, their flesh bulging through the gaps between adjacent sections of cord. He knotted the rope in front once more, over her belly where it sunk in. Claire was by now feeling most uncomfortable, as if she were wearing a corset which was much too constricting. He paused in his work to cast an eye briefly over the other activities; Jocelyn was now sucking and licking Jeremy's balls as he rolled his cock over her cheek and Sophronia was being divested of her golden gown.

Turning his head back to Claire, whose discomfort was more than compensated for by the sight of the wanton activity around her, Petrovski said, 'Was it not remarked upon that when you are to cane your girls you have them bend their bodies over the back of a chair?'

She wetted her lips. 'That is my custom,' she confessed.

'Then, slattern, you are about to discover how it is to be so positioned – and rather more.'

He had her get down from the table. Her arms were free; the rope was only binding her breasts and torso. Taking her over to the solid, oak chair at the head of the table he made her bend over its back, forcing her, with his hand shoving at the nape of her neck, to double over as far as she was able, so that her belly fat was creased into two rolls by the top of the chairback. Pulling the rope taut from its knot just above her navel – the knot itself half-buried in flesh – he secured first one wrist then the other to the tops of the front chairlegs.

Sophronia was by now half naked; her fabulous dress was an untidy pile on the floor, her lace bodice in disarray, and her tiny knickers pulled scruffily down to reveal her pubis almost entirely. Aubrey, with a good, thick hard-on – impressive enough to make Sophronia forgive him his other physical drawbacks – bouncing around as he completed the task of removing his trousers, had a beady eye on the performance of his girlfriend; Jeremy's cock was firmly planted between Jocelyn's scarlet lips, his trousers and pants hung at his knees and the tails of his jacket were draped over Sophronia's forearms, her hands clasping and fingernails clawing into his heavy, heaving, rudely exposed buttocks.

Aubrey now, naturally, craved the attentions of Sophronia's sweet mouth; but somehow Jeremy had omitted to inform him of the house rules. Kicking his trousers free from where they were caught over one foot, he grasped his member and moved his genitals into Sophronia's face. Until this moment there had been utter compliance from Lady Brexford. Now she put a hand, palm forwards, flat in front of her mouth and when Aubrey's glans touched it she pushed it firmly away.

'What's this?' he asked, puzzled.

'I'm sorry,' said Sophronia and meaning it, for she would dearly have loved to take that fine tool between her lips, 'it's not allowed.'

'Not allowed? How's that – not allowed?' Aubrey repeated. He looked at Jeremy and Jocelyn. 'But your husband is having a fine time being gobbled by my Josie.'

'Jeremy will not have it. He would punish me unmercifully.'

'But I fail to understand it. Here we all are' – he

169

glanced down at himself and at her state of partial undress, then at Alexis completing the bondage of the naked Miss Petty, then again at Jeremy's heaving bottom – 'sporting like this, in the midst of an orgy, and my prick may not pass your lips?'

'Unless he cares to change the rules,' said Sophronia, hopefully. 'Jeremy?'

Her husband turned his head to her. His face was strained, cheek muscles taut, eyes drooping, sure signs that he was hovering near to orgasm and holding himself back. Perhaps, Sophronia thought, in such a condition he might relax his annoying rule. 'What is it?' he grunted.

'Aubrey wishes me to fellate him.'

Jeremy blinked rapidly. Facial tension slackening, he slid his cock from Jocelyn's lips. 'Hell, Aubrey, I forgot to tell you,' he muttered. 'My guests may do anything they please with my wife save putting their dicks into any of her orifices – which are strictly reserved for myself.'

'Bit off, old boy,' Aubrey responded testily. 'I have allowed you, after all, full access to my girlfriend.'

'It's the way it has to be. My fault entirely for failing to inform you. I will leave Jocelyn alone now, should you wish.'

'Bit bloody late for that,' Aubrey grumbled. Sophronia, disappointed but unsurprised, attempted to save the potentially explosive situation by sturdily grabbing his cock and jerking her fist on it. Standing, she pulled her knickers to her knees and, tall as Aubrey in her high heels, closed in on him. She parted her thighs as far as the stretch in her knickers would allow and slipped his meaty shaft under her damp pussy, enclosing its back with her lips and its sides with her hot thigh tops.

'Surely you enjoy this?' she said softly, reaching to take hold of his balls, squeezing, and gently rocking her hips.

He grinned weakly, capitulating. 'But of course I like it. But I nevertheless fail to understand.'

'My husband is a most complicated man. Enjoy me as far as you may. You can take your opportunity later to fuck Claire Petty's face, and fanny – and bottom hole too if you are so inclined.'

Claire was now most securely attached to her chair, trussed so completely, the rope drawn so tight that she had no possibility of movement save in her extremities. The chair was open-backed with several horizontal struts, which had enabled the Count to wind both ends of the rope all the way down each of Claire's parted thighs and on down to her ankles; he had made such a thorough job of this that she appeared almost to be wearing silken rope stockings. With her head lifted, she had been staring through her tumbling hair at the other four, so excited by their activities that she had hardly noticed her discomfort. Now Alexis perversely took this distraction away from her by wrapping a black satin scarf around her eyes and tying it tightly, so that her world went utterly dark.

Satisfied with his expert handiwork, Count Petrovski now set about stripping himself naked, laying each item of his clothing carefully over a vacant chair. This done, he wrapped an ascetic hand around his handsomely lean hard-on, bent slightly at the knees behind his victim and commenced rubbing its head over her freckly behind, indenting little circular paths in the soft flesh.

Miss Petty was perfectly, grossly exposed. Each rope's length had been brought around her waist from her wrists, knotted at her back then dragged between her buttocks before beginning its tense spiral downwards from the very tops of her thighs; this had the interesting effect of stretching open both her vagina and her anus.

The Count began stroking his glans firmly up and down Claire's buttock cleft, pressing it at the entrance to her bottom hole each time he passed. A back door man by preference, and hugely aroused by his act of bondage, he found the inviting little hole a temptation resistable for only a very short space of time. He would castigate this deserving backside later; first he was going to indulge in some buggery, perhaps even release his sperm up there – the subsequent flagellation would in any case soon bring him up again for a more lasting debauch. The slenderness of his cock often permitted comfortable entry if lubricated by a copious dose of spittle; should he experience any difficulty easing it in Claire's bottom, he had his tin of petroleum jelly in a jacket pocket. He spat on the palm of a hand and wet his hard-on thoroughly. Then he covered the tips of two fingers with spittle and reached for his objective.

Claire Petty found herself in by far the most salacious situation of her life. She regretted the blindfold, never having had the opportunity to witness such acts as were now taking place feet from her; nevertheless, the fact of being trussed in an outrageously vulgar position – so tightly that she began to tingle and throb all over – and of being in the dark, utterly powerless to prevent her companions from doing anything they wished with her, was a massive turn-on. Instinct told her that it was the Count's cock so crudely teasing her – though it might have been his rigid fingers – and when it was replaced by wet fingertips poking and turning within her arsehole, she was perfectly aware for what reason the Count was thus lubricating her.

A thrill of the utmost raunchiness coursed through her bowels. For though it had been a frequent masturbatory fantasy of hers, Miss Petty had never been sodomised. The fingers were withdrawn to lodge the glans at her opening. Lean, hungry hands roughly grasped her roped tits. The Count doubled his long and lanky body over hers and began to push.

At first the pain made Claire draw in her breath in a great, noisy rush. But the headmistress had an accommodating behind and her sphincter proved most flexible, giving way easily. With less trouble than he had expected, Alexis slid his prick two-thirds of its length into Claire's back passage. He held himself still a moment, crumpling her breasts in his hands as if they were great, white, imprisoned sponges. Withdrawing to his glans he paused, then recommenced, burying his cock all the way up her to its root, his balls crushing against her pussy.

Miss Petty instantly understood the compelling pleasure of buggery. She felt crammed full as never before, the meat in her backside splendidly hot and silky in its rubberiness, doing something to her which by its very forbidden nature added to the ribald stirrings of her libido. Her sphincter performed a series of involuntary contractions, thereby spurring the Count on. He began to bum-ball her most vigorously, whilst his greedy eyes flicked from his reaming cock to the shameless behaviour on either side of the table and back down to the fat, white, freckled buttocks.

Lord Brexford, having heard no further complaints from Aubrey Taff, now had his gorgeous girlfriend with her knickers at her knees and her skirt heaped over her hips, bent double over the tabletop, one hand closed over a pear in a fruit bowl as he treated her to a hearty fucking; like Alexis, he had opted for a speedy climax at this stage of the proceedings in order to enjoy the sensualism of protracted arousal a littler later, when they all got down to the business of giving Miss Petty – in terms of both penetration and punishment – as much as any woman was equipped to take.

With panties halfway between hips and knees, bodice undone and tits jiggling, Sophronia was perched on Aubrey's knee as they steadily masturbated one another. Sensing that Aubrey, like herself, was close to coming, her hand found the back of Jocelyn's on the pear. Although she could not actually witness Claire's sodomisation directly because the headmistress's chair faced the table, being well aware of the Count's preferences she assumed that that was what was happening. The idea, as she watched Claire's upraised, ravaged face – which rolled from side to side as if in ecstatic denial of her plight – and Petrovski's hairy, jerking belly, spurred her on to orgasm. Her fist jumped on the prick in its grasp with the speed of a pounding hammer whilst her thighs thumped on Aubrey's busily frigging hand.

Leching at the sight of his girlfriend, her cheek flattened on the table next to the silver platter of uncarved suckling pig, which wore Claire's knickers about its head, who was getting it soundly thrown into her by Jeremy Brexford, Aubrey could contain himself no longer. His loins went through a series of small heaves which bounced Sophronia up and down as semen shot from him, spurting to the height of his chin, arching, and splattering down, narrowly missing the pig.

Communal carnality induced collective orgasm. Sophronia's hand tightened over Jocelyn's whose fingers pressed into and broke the skin of the pear. Pear juice oozed along with pussy juice, as Jeremy flooded Jocelyn's cunt. Only Alexis pumped on, protracting his enjoyment of Claire's backside for several more lusty thrusts before, with fiercely gritted teeth and a swinish grunt, he let fly inside it. Thus soiled, Claire, her G-spot aroused from an unaccustomed angle, her dirty mind thrilling at her lurid predicament, climaxed with a wail which was in part pain, as the Count's tit-grasping hands squeezed her hard enough to milk her as his balls erupted into her bowels.

Trousers and underpants bunched around his ankles, Jeremy lazily rolled away from Jocelyn's behind, his wet and wilting cock flopping from her pussy, and sank down into a chair, head drooping, breathing raspily. Count Petrovski remained sodomistically linked with Claire Petty, most of his weight pressing down onto her soft hips, his hands no longer assaulting her breasts but limp on the seat of the chair. The other three wallowed in their post-orgasmic state as they were, Sophronia with a hand on Aubrey's shrinking cock, the other over Jocelyn's on the pear, and with two of Aubrey's fingers nervelessly jammed in her pussy.

After a while Lord Brexford raised his head to break the steamy silence. Sounding pleased with himself he drawled, 'What a wonderfully depraved bunch we are. And the best is yet to come.' He reached for a wine bottle, filled a goblet and, putting it to his lips, drank thirstily, claret trickling down his chin. The others – with the exception of Miss Petty, who was unable – began to take lethargic notice as Jeremy stripped off his shoes, pants and trousers and stood up to remove his tailcoat. As he untied his bow and began to unbutton his shirt he said, 'Let's all get bare-arsed naked.' His eye fell on Jocelyn who had straightened up from the table; her dress had dropped, hiding her half-mast knickers. He laughed. 'Properly fucked, yet completely dressed. It won't do Josie!'

Nude, Jeremy threw back more wine as he fixed a crooked, evil smile on Miss Petty. He topped up his goblet, filled another to the brim and approached the helpless headmistress. 'How are you feeling, dear lady?' he asked her, resting a goblet on one of her buttocks as Count Petrovski finally uncoupled from her to wander towards the fire. 'I see you've had your bum well buggered – like a dick up it, do you?'

Claire groaned quietly. Recovering from her orgasm, she was becoming more aware by the second of her discomfort; she was cramped, the ropes were biting, and she longed to move. She also craved to set eyes on her companions, understanding from Jeremy's words that they were probably all stripping naked. But neither freedom from bondage, nor sight, was she to be granted; instead, another shock.

'Perhaps you would enjoy a sip of wine?' Jeremy asked, and held a goblet to her lips. She raised her head and opened her mouth, and he tipped a little of the claret into it. But he allowed her only what he had offered – a sip. He then took it from her mouth, held both goblets, one over each of her buttocks, and poured their entire contents over them.

The unexpectedness of the action caused her to shriek. As wine seeped into the rope around her thighs and ran down her sloping back into her hair, Jeremy guffawed loudly. Putting the empty goblets on the table he took hold of a full, opened bottle of claret – of which there were several – and poured it all over her. 'Excellent vintage,' he chuckled, 'good for the skin, no doubt.'

Hardly threatening, this action, but nevertheless subtle degradation in its way. The wine poured into Claire's hair at the nape of her neck and soaked down through her trailing locks to drip on the leather seat of the chair; it ran in rivulets over her shoulders and down her arms and trickled down her buttock cleft to wet a bottom hole stretched and a little sore from its battering; it seeped into the side of the satin scarf which bound her eyes; somehow it even found its way as far as her feet.

And that was merely the start. When the others were naked they and Count Alexis, laughing tipsily at their sport, surrounded the headmistress and together they each upended an entire bottle over her, saturating her ropes and drenching her hair. She accepted all of this without a word of protest, the only truly disagreeable part of it being the stickiness of the claret in her hair.

When they were done they were all merrily excited; a bunch of children who had been bullyingly naughty – and who were now about to be very bad. From a shadowy corner of the room Lord Brexford produced three matching items of the utmost significance, handing one each to the eager Alexis and Aubrey. They were willow wicker carpet beaters, each roughly the size and shape of a tennis racket and extremely pliable.

Sophronia meanwhile, whilst looking forward to what was to happen next, also had her sights on a rather different kind of diversion. Having enjoyed the intimacy of holding her hand as they were both brought to climax by their male partners, she now craved to possess the lithely superb body which Jocelyn had bared. She took hold of the girl's hand once more and drew her aside, determined to test her reaction to a lesbian advance. As her husband stooped to loosen Claire's blindfold, Sophronia gently brushed her lips against Jocelyn's; the response was immediate and most encouraging. The girl mashed her mouth against hers and crushed her delightful body into hers.

Mutual passion and arousal were instant. Sophronia wanted to take this tasty morsel in comfort; breaking off the kiss she breathed, 'Over there, where we can enjoy the fun – and one another.' She put her hand on Jocelyn's waist and took her to a sofa which was set diagonally across a corner of the room; here they lay down in each other's arms amongst silken cushions, kissing and at the same time watching expectantly as the men closed in on Miss Petty.

Cocks in various stages of re-erection, Lord Brexford, Count Petrovski and Aubrey Taff surrounded Claire Petty. Jeremy removed the wine soaked scarf from her eyes which went very wide as, looking around her, she saw the implements which each of the men clasped.

'So, Miss Wanker, Miss Flagellator,' Jeremy hissed sneeringly, 'you are about to discover what a truly severe thrashing is like.' He slammed his carpet-beater down and it hit the table top with a loud, sharp crack; a fork jumped and a goblet wobbled. 'This is to be a fitting revenge for all the poor, abused young wenches of Chalmers Finishing School.'

Claire's lower lip trembled. The sudden revelation of those three handsome cocks and the beaters in their owners' hands sent a spasm of utmost wantonness through her. But whilst craving a good drubbing she worried that they were about to do her serious damage.

'You don't intend to flay the skin off me – please?' she begged.

'You are about to be on the receiving end of the trouncing of your – and perhaps anyone's life,' Jeremy calmly told her, whilst actually having no intention of inflicting truly violent injury upon her. 'However, we will show you a limited amount of mercy – only to the extent which you do to your girls.'

'The lady is in any case extremely well padded,' noted the Count, eye on the chubby surrounds of the hole of his recent penetration. 'Such flesh is made to withstand a thorough flogging.' He paused. 'If no one objects, I shall strike the first blow.'

Alexis slid from her field of vision and Claire gritted her teeth, her gaze concentrated on Jeremy's rising penis. She heard a swish, her bottom exploded with pain and she yelped loudly.

'Well may you shout. Until you are hoarse, you may shout,' rasped Jeremy and he, too, moved behind her to lay his wicker torturer sturdily over the patchwork of angry marks which had already appeared on her buttocks. She yelled.

'Here, suck this up meanwhile; that will stop your pretty mouth,' said Aubrey. Supporting himself with a hand on the table edge, he swung his loins towards her and bent at the knees to poke his prick at her lips. She opened her mouth and willingly swallowed as Count Petrovski's arm rose and fell strongly once more.

It took but one more blow on her buttocks for the perverted headmistress to begin to enjoy the pain, and that, plus the cock which rapidly swelled between her lips filled her belly with a raging fire. As the mis-used carpet-beaters slammed into the wobbling flesh of Claire's behind, all three cocks quickly achieved full stands. Aubrey desisted from fucking her face to take Jeremy's place at her rear end to treat her by now very rosy buttocks to the first of many whacks to come; meanwhile Jeremy insisted his dangling, hairy balls one at a time into her mouth, followed by his engorged prick – which she sucked with a ferocity inspired by her beating.

Jocelyn had quickly proved to be every bit as horny a lover of the delights of the female pleasure ground as Sophronia herself. With the banquet hall filled with the provocative sounds of springy, woven willow larruping pudgy buttock flesh, Sophronia and Jocelyn indulged in a banquet of their own. Head to tail on the sofa with their faces buried between one another's splayed, smooth and lovely thighs, they feasted on each other's cunts with a wolfish appetite, their lesbian hunger spurred on by the background of loud, echoing slaps, grunts and moans.

The victim of a hiding harsher by far than any she had ever administered herself, Claire Petty wallowed in its painful pleasure. Further inflamed by her bondage, her mouth filled with one cock after another as the men revolved around her to take their turns at beating and being blown, she was happily wracked with orgasm upon orgasm.

Seething with the dark emotions of their vice, turgid, saliva-damp pricks swinging and swaying, the bestial three thrashed Miss Petty until her entire buttock area was glowing as puffily red as an overripe tomato. Finally Jeremy, fearing that the skin would soon begin to split, called a reluctant halt. The Count got in one final, mighty blow before his second climax of the evening rushed over him; he dropped the beater, took his cock in hand and directed its sudden gush of semen all over the afflicted area. Almost immediately, Jeremy erupted, his sperm hitting her hip and side as Aubrey let go his load in Claire's mouth, all of which she greedily swallowed.

The beautiful, wantonly entwined female bodies on the sofa shuddered from head to foot in ecstatic orgasm. Tongue tips stilled inside oozing, satisfied pussies at the same time as Aubrey's cock slipped, dripping, from Claire's lips and he straightened his legs to flatten his bare backside on the edge of the table, where he sagged. The other two men, deflated after their excesses, sweaty and panting, sank tiredly into chairs. Claire Petty's head dropped, her neck heavily stretching as she expressed all the feeling of what she had been through in a nervously shaking, protracted howl.

With the exception of Sophronia and Jocelyn who, after their mutual climax had rapidly reverted to a face to face embrace and were kissing tenderly, recovery was slow. Jeremy was the first of the men to revive. He drank more wine. He smacked his lips. His eyes wandered around the enticingly shadowy banquet hall, dwelt reflectively on the sorry state of the trussed headmistress, then shifted to the loving exhibition of lesbianism on the sofa. Delighted to detect yet more stirrings in his loins, he smiled; the night was young.

Claire Petty produced a lingering groan. She raised her heavy head to peer around her. Sexual thirsts quenched, she was beginning to feel the full consequences of her predicament. She was badly cramped. The rope which scrunched her breasts, bit into her belly and pinched the flesh of thigh and forearms was hurting her. But above all her poor bottom, throbbing painfully in time with her heartbeat, felt as if it had grown to twice its size – though it was merely slightly bloated. Her eyes caught those of her principal tormentor. 'Release me now, My Lord, I beg of you,' she pleaded.

His gaze swept over her utterly abused body in cynical amusement. She was stained with wine, her lank hair drenched, her bindings a patchy, claret red. All over the fat orbs of her behind were the outpourings of Count Petrovski's testicles, a stark, creamy-white contrast to the crimson flesh. Jeremy's own semen was splashed down her side and had trickled onto the tabletop. The degradation had been most thorough, yet could not truly be classed as degradation at all since Miss Petty had derived enormous, gross and ribald pleasure from it. Well, mused Lord Brexford, it was fitting that she should now suffer properly for a while.

'You will remain in your present position, but untouched by hand or cock or paddle, until we five have desported ourselves some more,' he told her calmly, a flat smile on his lips. 'You may watch us – but whatever fresh cravings our behaviour induces in you will remain unsatisfied. Should you protest, you will be firmly gagged – so kindly desist. Later, before your release, you will solemnly promise that once, after tomorrow evening, I have done with Ellie Branks, you will send me another lass, equally as succulent.'

'But I can promise you that now,' gasped the headmistress. 'I . . . I'm truly hurting.'

'Hurt on,' responded Jeremy, cruelly. Getting to his feet, he wandered across the room to his wife and the lovely Jocelyn.

Chapter Ten

A keen edge of anticipation adding to her enjoyment of the day, Sophronia Brexford – with the help of Alexis Petrovski – spent much of Saturday putting the finishing touches to a cellar which she had been preparing, bit by bit, for a definitive, perverse purpose, for several weeks. Her interest in the black arts had been absorbing her lately almost as much as sex; tonight was to be the culmination of her training.

Ellie Branks, meanwhile, passed that same day a bundle of libidinous nerves; memories of the evening of her defloration and dissipation with the lord of the hill and his fine lady were as fresh as if it had just happened; wicked thoughts of what might further befall her the coming night crowded her mind. All day she was itchily aware of her needful little pussy. She had scratched the itch once in the toilet with a furtively hurried masturbation, but it had done little to relieve it. As the appointed time for her to be picked up and driven to Deal Manor drew closer, so her earthy agitation increased.

Once again Lord Brexford employed the banquet hall and the string quartet, but his elaborate plans for this evening were very different from those of the one before. When Ellie, cloaked in nerves as plainly as if they were woven about her, arrived it was not, as she had rather expected, as a solitary guest for the second time.

The night had cleared and there was a full moon. The house was bright, light bursting from almost every window and music faint, but gay, came from within as the girl was shown up the steps to the front doors.

Escorted by a butler into the banquet hall, wearing the same blue satin dress as before – she had nothing else suitable, for Chalmers was not an establishment whose young ladies were expected to go galivanting around during the evenings – she was amazed to discover that a number of people were merrily waltzing there.

Sophronia, dazzling in heaps of white lace chiffon, took immediate charge of Ellie, fussing around her briskly and introducing her to many of the members of what Ellie little knew was perhaps the most dissolute crowd ever to have gathered beneath the ancient roof of the manor. Among them were the loose and lovely profligates, Millie and Lettice, Jeremy's London mistress, Charlotte – of whose relationship with her husband Sophronia had no idea – the raunchy novelist, Edwin Smythe-Parker, Count Petrovski, the mincing ballet dancer and musician Arnold, and Aubrey Taff with the delectable Jocelyn. There were some twenty more people, all splendidly attired in evening clothes.

Judging by how they were dressed and the way in which the guests were comporting themselves they might have been some of the most respectable luminaries in the land rather than an extraordinary collection of hedonists, libertines, perverts – and practitioners of witchcraft. Only about half of them had ever attended a similar event to the one which was planned for later that evening, but all – all, that

was, except Ellie – were aware of what it was to con-
sist of, and were looking forward to it with great relish and enthusiasm; sex and the black arts were well
known to go happily hand in hand.

Unbeknown to Ellie, her arrival was a signal for
the dancing to end shortly and a feast – meant to be
almost Bacchanalian – to begin. As she took her seat
with Lord Brexford on her left at the head of table
and Sophronia across from her, Ellie found that
though her nervousness was largely gone, the close
proximity of Sophronia and Jeremy had the effect of
exacerbating her sexual longing.

The assembly ate and drank their way, very nearly
to excess, through a sumptuous spread. There was
joviality in the air, but it seemed false and overlaid
with a certain amount of tension. Each time that Ellie
glanced down the table, she got the impression that
there were more eyes studying her than was natural,
that there was speculation in them, that people were
slyly discussing her; somehow she was certain that
not all of this was in her imagination.

Neither Jeremy nor Sophronia made any verbal al-
lusions to their sexual encounter with Ellie, but the
significant, speculative way in which they kept looking at her, their occasional light touching of her hand,
her arm, her knee or her thigh and brushings of their
feet against hers, said more than words. By the meal's
end, plied with wine and having had her first ever
taste of brandy, Ellie was feeling as if there were some
fiercely wild sex animal in her loins fighting to escape
– and she was thus, as her hosts had intended, fully
primed for the evening ahead.

Lord Brexford took a final sip at his coffee, swallowed some brandy, and stood up. He rattled a solid
silver knife against an empty wine bottle to call atten-

tion to himself and, as silence ensued, proclaimed loudly: 'My friends, the time has arrived. You may all now like to prepare for the – um – festivity. My wife and Count Petrovski will show you the way.' He retook his seat, watching in satisfied amusement and holding onto Ellie's upper arm, as the company noisily made their way from the hall Then they were alone except for the string quartet which was playing a piece from Strauss.

His droopy, wanton, brown eyes invaded Ellie's sexual soul, his strong, experienced fingers her breast as Jeremy quietly said, 'Alone at last, little Ellie. Alone at last.'

'But where . . .?' She was about to ask him where the rest had gone but he stilled her question with a finger on her lips.

'Come.' Taking her hand he rose, pulled her to her feet and led her across the hall in a different direction than the others had taken, through a door. They ascended a broad and chilly stone staircase, where the only light was from a single candle at each turn in the stairs, then he led her along a dim passage to his bedroom – next to Sophronia's – where a servant had been checking every half an hour to see that the coal fire was well stoked up and brightly burning. In welcome contrast to the stairs and passageways the room was comfortably warm; it was very much a man's bedroom, filled with sporting prints and hunting trophies. But Ellie was given little time to study it because as soon as Jeremy had closed and locked the door, he folded her into his arms, staring down into her pale blue eyes which, faintly glazed from drinking, searched his with restless expectancy.

'I have been waiting most impatiently for this moment all evening,' he said softly.

Ellie became very bold. 'And I all week,' she replied, sounding very grown up to herself.

He kissed her with a passion rooted in lust for her young, pliable body, for her splendid tits and lovely, round behind, for her fleshy little almost-virgin pussy – assailed by no man but himself – and he succeeded during the long and racy clash of lips and mingling of tongues to fondle and grope all of those yearned-for places and in so doing, to turn Ellie's insides to jelly. Then he led her to his bed and sat her on its green, Indian silk cover.

Prepared for, hoping for, expecting, Lord Brexford to undress her, Ellie discovered, with a thrilling shock, that for the moment he had different plans. With his hands on her shoulders, their fierce grip betraying his sexual impatience, he muttered, 'Do you remember that when last we were together, in my wife's bedroom, after you ceased to be a virgin, that Sophronia demonstrated on me one of the most exciting ways in which to stimulate a man?'

She recalled only too vividly. Gazing up over his frilled evening shirt front and floppy, maroon bow tie into narrowed eyes where lust crowded out all other expression, she said, 'When she, when she took it, took it in . . .?' she found herself unable to finish the sentence.

'In her mouth, yes,' Jeremy finished for her. 'I want you to do that. Will you do that, please Ellie?'

She said nothing. A delicious shiver ran through her. Her eyes slid, with a certain amount of raunchy apprehension back down the shirt and over the single, fastened button of his tailcoat to where the cutaway front of the jacket revealed the bottom half of a paisley cummerbund; below it, the silken crotch of his evening trousers bulged dramatically. She hesitated, for a moment close to panic yet keen to do his bidding. She wetted her lips.

He took her hand and placed it over the bulge, strongly pressing the backs of her delicate fingers. 'For you, little girl,' he whispered, 'for nobody else but you.' Stripping off his jacket, he threw it onto the bed then reached behind his back to unfasten the cummerbund.

The only male organ Ellie had so far known felt solid, hard and inviting, its warmth seeping, through the double layer of silk trousers and underpants which enclosed it, into her quavering palm. As the cummerbund fell to the floor and Jeremy began to unfasten his fly buttons he said, thickly, 'I'll do these. Then you the underpants.'

She took her hand away, watching, transfixed, pussy afire, as opened black silk revealed white silk beneath. Both her hands came to a momentary rest on his muscular thighs, the trouser top dropped loosely over them; she pulled them away and the slippery material concertinaed to Jeremy's ankles. His hard-on which, encased before her eyes in shiny white, was digging sideways, a great, potent length of rigid flesh, seemed to Ellie far more daunting than when hidden by trouser front. 'Go on,' he insisted, with a tiny jerk of his hips, 'get it out.'

There were but three small metal buttons on the tight pants, which Ellie unfastened with trembly fingers; while she was still trying to summon up the courage to dip her hand amongst the forest of curly hair and penis root exposed, Jeremy impatiently folded the pants down over his thighs. His cock sprang into view, waving briefly at Ellie's face and stilling, its swollen head inches from her lips. She gazed at it in hypnotic fascination, hands again flattened on his thighs over the inside-out pants, damp lips slightly apart. But she could not quite find the courage to do what he wanted her to – and what her panting libido demanded of her.

Jeremy's hand reached for the nape of her neck, fingers slipping through her shiny, blonde hair. He pulled her head forward until his glans touched the desired, pouty-pink lips. 'Open your mouth, girl,' he demanded hoarsely. As she did, his cockhead sank into it, stretching her lips wide, and tasting not unpleasantly salty.

As his hips began a gentle rocking and three inches of Lord Brexford's sturdy, warm prick slid back and forth within her mouth, Ellie's eyes fixed on the mass of moving pubic hair; her hands crept around taut buttocks to grasp them firmly. But as yet she was so shocked by the mere fact of what she was doing that she was deriving little pleasure from the act – though her pussy remained as needful as ever.

'Suck,' Jeremy commanded. 'Suck like a calf at an udder – and handle my testicles, do.'

Containing himself commendably – though he would dearly have loved to have built up to orgasm and come in Ellie's sweet mouth – Jeremy gave her a crash course in fellatio. The shock gradually subsided. By the time she had learned to lick his balls, to take them one at a time into her mouth, to flicker her tongue over his cock as she wanked it, to tease its tiny hole with her tongue-tip, Ellie was thoroughly enjoying this wanton game, and her knickers were very wet indeed.

Arriving at the stage where any further schooling of this virgin mouth was very likely to cause him to come, with a supreme effort of will Jeremy forced himself to break away from her, as another lickerish idea occurred to him. As he went to a wardrobe, she watched his buttocks with a certain amount of regret; the cock-sucking had proved most agreeable to her, arousing her to giddy, libidinous heights. Suddenly a new, wicked thrill shuddered through her as Lord Brexford returned to the bed with a riding crop in his hand.

'Now I shall treat you to a few swipes with this,' he said, with an evil grin. He slapped the plaited leather and sprung steel with its tiny knots at the tip into his palm. 'Because I know how much you like it, and because dirty-minded young ladies deserve punishment. Then we two will fuck – speedily. We shall indulge in what is vulgarly referred to as a quickie in order to somewhat relieve our needs. After which, we shall join the others.'

Ellie was the softest of putty in the libertine lord's hands. Her lips were drooling and she was panting quietly, her eyes droopy and foggy with sexual craving. When Jeremy took her shoulder in his rough hand, spun her around and flung her violently face down across his bed, she hit it with a drawn out whimper of anticipatory excitement. Grabbing her skirt by its scrunched hem, he heaved it up her legs and over her back as if ripping open a curtain. And rip was exactly what he did to her baggy green school knickers as he dragged them down to her knees. He stumbled and nearly fell with his trousers around his ankles and kicked his feet out of them, hard-on swinging and swaying; then he raised the crop and with a grunt swiped it down across Ellie's buttocks.

Six times he whacked the tender bottom which had barely recovered from Miss Petty's caning; six stinging, cutting blows, the riding crop whistling each time through the air to paint a thin and vivid red stripe across cringing buttock flesh. And six times, savouring every moment of her beating, Ellie screeched.

Done, aroused beyond containment, Jeremy flung the crop across the room and fell upon Ellie's inflamed backside with an animal roar. He fisted his prick beneath her buttocks and into her soaking little cunt, pounding into her with such a fury that he brought himself, and her, to orgasm in less than a minute.

Panting, sweating, impaled in Ellie up to his balls, Lord Brexford lay on her back as she quietly sobbed beneath him with the relief her climax had brought to a pussy which had been most desperate. There he remained, until his cock had shrunk to its flaccid state, then he heaved himself off her to swing his feet to the floor. Drained eyes resting on her bare, red-lined backside, he jabbed two fingers into the recipient of his sperm as he muttered, 'Now we prepare for Sophronia's fun and games.'

From the wardrobe Jeremy produced two heavy, cotton robes, one white, one black. Dropping the white one on the bed next to Ellie – who lay in the same position in which she had been whipped and fucked, skirt piled on her back, knickers at her knees, head cradled in her arm – he said, 'Strip yourself naked and put that on.' He took off his tailcoat, threw it on the bed, and began to unbutton his shirt.

Ellie rolled over and sat up with an 'Ouch!' as her stinging buttocks made contact with the cold silk bedspread. Without questioning the reason for it, she peeled her dress over her head, got out of her knickers, stood up, and put the robe on. It was slightly too big for her; its hem trailed on the floor, its wide sleeves reached her knuckles. There was a tasselled cord which she pulled around her waist to tie its end in a bow. She did not realise that there was a cowl hanging down her back until Jeremy, clad in his black robe – also with a cowl at its neck – pulled it up and over her head. Voluminous, the cowl reached so far forward that it cloaked her face in dark shadow. Jeremy then produced leather sandals from somewhere and they both put them on.

Ellie at last asked, nonchalantly – she was looking forward to more sex no matter what form it might take – why they were dressed in that fashion.

He half-filled a brandy glass and handed it to her, not answering her question at first. 'Drink that down,' he said, 'take your time. You will find it good for nerves which will perhaps need a little steeling for what we are about to get involved in.'

'Oh.' She was visited by a hollow feeling of doubt. The glass all but disappeared within the cowl before it touched her lips. She swallowed, then she spluttered, despite the fact that the liquer was a fine and mellow vintage. 'Involved?' she repeated quietly.

'My wife has lately taken a keen interest in the matters of sorcery. To please her, though I believe it to be nonsense, I have encouraged her. For instance, I helped her with the arrangements for her first satanic mass this evening.' Lord Brexford peered into the shadow of the cowl as he saw that Ellie had gone very still at his words. 'But it's quite all right, dear girl. It will be no more than an elaborate game. Essentially a sex game.' He paused. 'Finish your brandy, then we'll go down.'

Before they left the bedroom, Jeremy lit the wick of an ornate, ceramic oil lamp. They descended the gloomy, twisting staircase they had climbed a short while previously, and crossed the great hall, which to Ellie seemed to have taken on a slightly forboding atmosphere since last she had seen it. He stopped them at the top of an unlit flight of stairs leading to the cellars, where he covered his head with the black cowl. 'You are not to be in the least alarmed,' he told her softly, 'no harm will come to you. But let me prepare you for what is to be. You, near as dammit a virgin, are to represent a symbol of purity, and as such you will be at the centre of the so-called mass. You will be expected to accommodate,' he paused, eyes glinting in the gloom of the cowl, his free hand finding her buttocks beneath her robe, fingers delving below them to dig into the softness of her pussy, '. . . a number of erect male organs during the course of this celebration.' He paused again, his fingers pushing and jiggling. 'I trust you will raise no objections?'

Ellie's head was beginning to spin from the brandy. Her single orgasm had failed to douse the fire in her loins more than temporarily, and it had begun to burn once more before they left the bedroom. Now Jeremy's words, and his probing fingers, had the effect of bringing her to a high pitch of excitement. Her reply to his question made itself clear by her whimper and protracted shudder. Pleased with this, Jeremy left her pussy alone, took her hand and, holding the lamp high, led her down the worn stone steps.

Pausing at one of many doors in a dank and featureless hall at the bottom, he murmured, 'The theory of my wife and certain other members of this mass is that defiling innocence is one of the aids to raising the Devil. You are innocence. No Devil, of course, will appear, so fear not.' He released her hand and opened the door.

They stepped into blackness and silence relieved only by a massive pinewood fire in a chimney almost twice the size of any other in the house at the far end of the cavernous cellar. Flames three feet high and as broad again at their communal base, roared, throwing out an orange glow, and the wood crackled and spat.

At first, as Jeremy closed the door, Ellie could make out nothing but the fire. He took her hand again and led her slowly into the cellar. She began to discern indistinct, vaguely human shapes, black against black, surrounding them at a short distance. They turned to their right, at a tangent to the fire, making for still more forms ahead.

Sophronia observed the progress of Jeremy and Ellie, the two of them clearly lit by the lamp Lord Brexford held above his head – a moving pool of light in a sea of darkness – with thumping heart. Her scene was set, the night was hers; her diabolical cellar, she felt, was to be a great success. She had had the ceiling painted black, the walls lined with black velvet and the floor covered in heavy black wool carpet. She was standing, still as death, trying not to breathe, next to Count Petrovski and behind a black velvet upholstered altar. At the altar's head was a human skull and a large, inverted, silver cross. Sophronia and Alexis were clad – as were all the other guests – in similar black, ankle-length, cowled robes to Jeremy. The lovely Ellie, though not quite purity unbesmirched, was the only person to be wearing white; she glided up to the altar like some phantom of the night.

Clinging on to Ellie's fragile hand, Lord Brexford stopped them two paces from the altar. She was still able to make out very little. Having been forewarned that there was nothing to be afraid of, she was nevertheless experiencing a nervous fluttering in her belly; the atmosphere, whether it was contrived as part of an elaborate game or no, was weird and very scary.

She clung to Jeremy's hand as if it was her last link with normality.

Ellie's arrival at the altar triggered off proceedings – as her appearance in the banquet hall had signalled the start of the feast. A shadowy figure, becoming clearer as it progressed, moved around the walls to light the low wicks of a series of oil lamps affixed there. When the entire cellar was bathed in a yellowish, steady glow, tempered by the dancing light of the fire, the figure – of indeterminate sex, as were they all with their faces buried in the shadow of cowls – ignited a candle inside the skull on the altar; the eye sockets glimmered into eerie life.

A mumbled chanting began, nearly incoherent, sounding like a prayer – which, of an infernal sort, it was. Only when she made out, coming from Sophronia's lips, the words, 'Oil with head my annointed . . .' did Ellie realise with shock that they were reciting the twenty-third psalm backwards.

Setting his lamp down at the altar's head between the skull and the inverted cross, Jeremy put his mouth to Ellie's ear and whispered, 'It falls on me now to arrange you on the altar. Fear nothing.'

Ellie was not about to overcome her nerves that easily, but lust was her dominant emotion. Jeremy's words at the head of the cellar stairs rang arousingly clear in her memory. She was 'expected to accommodate a number of erect male organs'. As she was eased down onto her back she realised with a thrill that this was where that event was to take place.

The altar was a cunning contrivance of Count Petrovski's made to his specifications by Lady Brexford's carpenters. It was five feet wide by eight feet long, with an oblong piece of two feet wide and three feet long missing from the end furthest from its head.

When Ellie was installed on her back, her head propped on a velvet cushion below the grisly mouth of the skull, at first her toes touched the floor, her legs within the oblong hole. Jeremy took her by the ankles, raised her legs, and laid each one on either side of the cut-out.

With eyes gone suddenly very wide, and biting her bottom lip to keep it from trembling, Ellie watched as, standing between her legs, Jeremy pulled undone the bow in her sash and opened her robe, letting it fall away to hang down and touch the carpet on either side of the altar – leaving only her shoulders and arms covered. Ellie, who had been until her recent, raunchy voyage of sexual discovery an innocent young lady with only uncertain dreams of sex, was all but naked, legs spread to open her pussy slightly, her body bathed in light from the oil lamp next to the skull for all to see. She felt very tiny, very vulnerable, scared, ashamed – and dreadfully horny, all at the same time.

Lord Brexford approached the head of the altar from where he stood looking down at Ellie's nude body. His hands on her shoulders were gentle and reassuring – not particularly because he was afraid for her but because the last thing he wanted was for any sudden panic on her part to spoil the evening.

The chanting increased in volume, speeding up as the psalm began again at its end – 'ever for Lord the of house . . .' – while Alexis Petrovski detached himself from Sophronia's side to slide – an over-tall, mysterious, scary monk – into the cut-out between Ellie's spread legs. He closed in on her bare, inviting little pussy. His long, pale hands alit on the insides of her milky thighs. His eyes, lost in darkness, became piggish. With her heart going wild, Ellie could not suppress a small squeal as she watched the Count hoist his robes to his waist to reveal his lanky, potent, hard-on.

The altar was built to the height of an average man's legs, the sole purpose of its evil design to provide comfortable sexual access to any woman prostrated upon it during satanic orgies. Not being such an average sized man, the Count was obliged to bend at the knees in order for his genitals to come down to the level of Ellie's. He pushed in the head of his cock and, finding Ellie's pussy wet and ready, shoved its length all the way up her. Her knees rose with a jerk. She gasped loudly as she gazed down through her trembling tits at the sight of only the second cock she had ever seen disappearing into her, seconds after first clapping eyes on it. Her fingers, hidden by the spread robe, clawed at the heavy velvet beneath them as the Count's prick moved slowly into her until their pubic bushes mingled, then slid out to its glans.

Thirteen times Petrovski plunged then, as Ellie was accustoming herself to and even beginning to relish this public fucking, he withdrew. He let his robes fall and rejoined Sophronia, resuming his chanting as he stared down at Ellie's nakedness.

Edwin Smythe-Parker, the wanton novelist, took Petrovski's place; the third prick of Ellie's life was exposed to her eyes only to plunge inside her pussy immediately. Emulating that of the Count, this sturdy cock rammed home into her thirteen times before being withdrawn.

'A number of erect male organs,' Lord Brexford had told her. He had not been specific. Exactly how many he had meant by that was sixteen, excluding his own. Ellie found herself in a world the existence of which she could never have imagined. Her head began to spin then went on spinning, her battered pussy experienced contraction after contraction. She hovered on the ecstatic brink of orgasm, all fear and shame forgotten as rampant, anonymous, cock after cock pounded her the ritualistically required thirteen times – the cabbalistic number of deep superstition, and the amount of people who traditionally comprise a witches' coven.

Lord Brexford took his turn between her legs the last, the only cock which she recognised – and the only one, in thirteen brief but massive thrusts which had his balls slamming into her buttocks, to bring her all the way off. As he banged into her for the eleventh time she wailed her climax, lifting her feet and wrapping them hard around his buttocks; he was obliged to prise them free in order to uncouple from her after his thirteenth plunge because she was gripping him so fiercely in the aftermath of her huge orgasm that he might have thrust again and ruined the ritual.

A change in proceedings. The chanting ceased. In the rustling silence the assembly got out of their robes and sandals. An abundance of naked white flesh presented itself in stark contrast to its utterly black background.

A mass orgy, Sophronia had been instructed by the expert Petrovski, under the conditions he and she would create, is a religious rite which should produce a trance-like state encouraging the appearance of the Devil himself. To this end, a larger area of floor across from the altar, adjoining a wall, was covered with a velvet upholstered, heavy foam mattress and scattered with black silk cushions. Upon this enormous bed the nude 'worshippers' gathered to fall upon one another's bodies with bawdy greed.

With the foam floor covered with an ocean of writhing copulation, and the air filled with a rising crescendo of gasps and grunts, moans and sighs, Jeremy elected to continue with his pleasure between Ellie's silken thighs at the altar. Naked now, he was not obliged to hold his robe up under his chest and his hands were free to rove and plunder as he heaved his cock steadily in and out of her. Having taken over-swift pleasure with the girl in his bedroom he now meant to draw this humping out for as long as possible. As he savoured every moment of screwing Ellie, his eyes travelled over a vista of mass rutting which was made that much more arousing defined as it was by its black background.

Sophronia, Jeremy noted, as his buttocks bounced and his hands squeezed Ellie's tits together, was obeying the house rules like a good wife. Knowing that it would be the worse for her later should she fail to comply, she had pounced upon AC/DC Arnold as her on-the-floor sexual partner. The two, the only couple not writhing around with genitals locked, were enthusiastically tossing one another off.

In a smutty-minded schoolgirl-dreamland, Ellie had her feet firmly crossed over the small of Lord Brexford's back. With no urging on from Jeremy, her index finger had somehow found its way into his bottom hole where it was buried to the second knuckle, as her hand rode back and forth with his behind. Her other hand clung tightly to his plunging balls as her eyes roved over the Rabelaisian scene on the floor.

It was almost a half an hour before Jeremy let himself go. He dragged his cock from Ellie's raging pussy to direct a stream of sperm over her, semen which had been under such mounting pressure in his balls that its initial spurt was so strong it arched right across her torso to fall on her cheek, then splash her lips and hit her neck before pouring onto her breasts and belly; the final drops mingled amongst her pubic hairs as she yelled an orgasm which echoed all around the cellar.

The orgy, sustaining itself, feeding upon itself, leched on; partners changed, semen flowed into every available female orifice and, from Count Petrovski, up Arnold's backside. A certain, euphoric, trance-like state was, indeed, induced in many of the debauchees as orgasm after orgasm rippled through the heaving carpet of flesh. Several participants even began to hallucinate.

Satan, however, stubbornly refused to put in an appearance.

'Do you realise something?' asked Lord Brexford of his lovely lady wife as, looking spruce, fresh, and utterly contented with life the two of them tucked into a hearty, noon breakfast the following day.

As she buttered a thin, crisp slice of toast, Sophronia turned an angelic smile upon him. 'I'm hardly a mind reader, darling.'

'I was merely about to remark that my acquaintanceship with Claire Petty seems to have added a most thrilling aspect to our sex lives.'

'Congratulating yourself on your initiative, are you?'

'Well, yes.'

Biting off an edge of the toast, Lady Brexford chewed thoughtfully. 'I wonder what delectable young trollop Miss Petty will provide us with next?'

'I wonder?' echoed her husband, jaw twitching.

NEW BOOKS

Coming up from Nexus and Black Lace

The Handmaidens by Aran Ashe
March 1995   Price: £4.99   ISBN: 0 352 32985 8
Aran Ashe, creator of the legendary Lidir books, is back with a brilliant new series of erotic fantasy novels: the Chronicles of Tormunil. In this, the first book, we meet Sianon and Iroise, young and beautiful serving wenches who seem condemned to a future of absolute obedience and self-denial in the sinister Abbey. Help may be at hand in the form of a handsome young traveller – but it's help at a price.

The Governess at St Agatha's by Yolanda Celbridge
March 1995   Price: £4.99   ISBN: 0 352 32986 6
A welcome return for Miss Constance de Comynge, former Cornish governess. Now she's headmistress of St Agatha's, a young ladies' academy where discipline is foremost on the syllabus. Competition is tough for places in the 'Swish Club', a select group whose beautiful members revel in punishing each other – and prominent members of the local gentry.

Lingering Lessons by Sarah Veitch
April 1995   Price: £4.99   ISBN: 0 352 32990 4
Leanne has just inherited an old boarding school, but she has to share it with the mysterious Adam Howard. Only one thing is certain about her new partner: he is a true devotee of corporal punishment. The last thing Leanne expects is to be drawn into his sordid yet exciting world, but the temptation proves irresistible.

The Awakening of Lydia by Philippa Masters
April 1995   Price: £4.99   ISBN: 0 352 33002 3
As the daughter of a district commissioner during the Boer War, Lydia has plenty of opportunity for excitement – and plenty of sex-starved men to pleasure her. But their skills are nothing compared to the voracious sexual appetites of the local tribesmen, who waste no time in taking the stunning sixteen-year-old captive.

Unfinished Business by Sarah Hope-Walker
March 1995   Price: £4.99   ISBN: 0 352 32983 1

Joanne's job as financial analyst for a leading London bank requires a lot of responsibility and control. Her true, submissive self has little opportunity to blossom until the suave, gifted and dominant Nikolai walks into her life. But her happiness is soon threatened by the return of an equally masterful old flame.

Nicole's Revenge by Lisette Allen
March 1995   Price: £4.99   ISBN: 0 352 32984 X

It's taken Nicole Chabrier four years' hard work at the Paris Opera to make something of herself. But when France erupts into revolution, she has to rely on a dashing stranger to save her from an angry mob. She is only too happy to use her considerable charms to repay the favour and to help Jacques gain revenge on those who wronged him.

Crimson Buccaneer by Cleo Cordell
April 1995   Price: £4.99   ISBN: 0 352 32987 4

Cheated out of her inheritance, Carlotta Mendoza wants revenge; and with her exquisite looks and feminine wiles, there is no shortage of men willing to offer her help. She takes to the seas with a rugged buccaneer and begins systematically boarding, robbing and sexually humiliating her enemies.

La Basquaise by Angel Strand
April 1995   Price: £4.99   ISBN: 0 352 32988 2

Oruela is a modern young woman of 1920s Biarritz who seeks to join the bohemian set. Her lover, Jean, is helping her to achieve her social aspirations. But an unfortunate accident involving her father brings her under suspicion, and a sinister game of sexual blackmail throws her life into turmoil . . .

NEXUS BACKLIST

All books are priced £4.99 unless another price is given. If a date is supplied, the book in question will not be available until that month in 1995.

CONTEMPORARY EROTICA

THE ACADEMY	Arabella Knight	
CONDUCT UNBECOMING	Arabella Knight	Jul
CONTOURS OF DARKNESS	Marco Vassi	
THE DEVIL'S ADVOCATE	Anonymous	
DIFFERENT STROKES	Sarah Veitch	Aug
THE DOMINO TATTOO	Cyrian Amberlake	
THE DOMINO ENIGMA	Cyrian Amberlake	
THE DOMINO QUEEN	Cyrian Amberlake	
ELAINE	Stephen Ferris	
EMMA'S SECRET WORLD	Hilary James	
EMMA ENSLAVED	Hilary James	
EMMA'S SECRET DIARIES	Hilary James	
FALLEN ANGELS	Kendal Grahame	
THE FANTASIES OF JOSEPHINE SCOTT	Josephine Scott	
THE GENTLE DEGENERATES	Marco Vassi	
HEART OF DESIRE	Maria del Rey	
HELEN – A MODERN ODALISQUE	Larry Stern	
HIS MISTRESS'S VOICE	G. C. Scott	
HOUSE OF ANGELS	Yvonne Strickland	May
THE HOUSE OF MALDONA	Yolanda Celbridge	
THE IMAGE	Jean de Berg	Jul
THE INSTITUTE	Maria del Rey	
SISTERHOOD OF THE INSTITUTE	Maria del Rey	

EROTIC SCIENCE FICTION

Please send me the books I have ticked above.

Name . . . .

Address . . . .

. . . .

. . . .

. . . . Post code . . . .

Send to: **Cash Sales, Nexus Books, 332 Ladbroke Grove, London W10 5AH.**

Please enclose a cheque or postal order, made payable to **Nexus Books,** to the value of the books you have ordered plus postage and packing costs as follows:

UK and BFPO – £1.00 for the first book, 50p for each subsequent book.

Overseas (including Republic of Ireland) – £2.00 for the first book, £1.00 for the second book, and 50p for each subsequent book.

If you would prefer to pay by VISA or ACCESS/MASTER-CARD, please write your card number and expiry date here:

. . . .

Please allow up to 28 days for delivery.

Signature . . . .